the Warp & the Weft

and other stories

Contents

I thank my family and friends who stood by me and made this book possible.

My sincere thanks to Rani Ray and Meenakshi Bharat for their valuable editorial contributions.

The Musk Deer

Durga Prasad looked around his rented flat in the metropolis. With his long legs, he had only to take a few strides to cover the entire flat. The hall, the bedrooms, and the kitchen together could not measure up to the rear veranda of his ancestral home. The bedroom window in his opulent house in the village, faced shady trees of jamun and the windows in this apartment overlooked the service lane, which separated another row of ugly flats. Looking across, he could see a mother pig and a baby pig, sitting idly on the garbage heap that lined the lane monotonously. The mother pig got up and shook itself free of the crow, which had comfortably settled on its back. What a funny sight! But Durga Prasad couldn't laugh. As a matter of fact, he had forgotten how to laugh. Why had he come so far away from his beautiful home to such an ugly flat? Beautiful home? Yes, it had been. Until recently. But now, it was a haunted house. The haunting presence of the absences: that was what had driven him away from home. The long corridors and the spacious verandas... The pattering feet of Mukund and Somu chasing each other. Behind the tall fluted pillars, little Somu playing hide and seek. Bharati, calling out to them in her shrill voice to come and have milk.

Bharati, you have not been in my thoughts for a while. Do you see the photograph on the mantelpiece? Mukund and Somu, tall and broad-shouldered, in their black coats and caps as law graduates. That was what you had dreamed for them. When Somu decided to give up his job in the city, I wasn't worried. Why should he slog in a firm for a petty boss? I had earned enough money for my sons, and there was enough work at home. All those books I published during the past two years, I couldn't have managed without Somu. What a way he had with words! My prosaic analyses of lawsuits and criminal cases, with a few touches here and there, he transformed into inspiring stories. I couldn't bear to enter the library. I had to close it down and seal it. I saw him everywhere: perched on the ladder, reaching out for books; sitting behind the tall lamp, bent over the manuscripts; stretched on the carpet, looking idly up at the ceiling... Oh! He was everywhere.

I couldn't look at the little boys and the housewives around the neighbourhood – they brought back a flood of memories. To the children, he was the big brother. He prepared badminton courts and football grounds for them. Every festival season, he would arrange cricket matches for them. He came back from his monthly visits to the town like Santa Claus carrying for each one of them, a gift: a paint brush, a mask or cartoons. And as for the women, he was their man Friday. He repaired their sluggish gadgets and fixed erring electrical points for them. And the servants adored him. Any medical problem, a quarrel with a neighbour, a land dispute, they would run to him. He had no enemies. Everyone loved him and he was so happy, so full of life. That is what intrigues me.

Why did he do it? Bharati, I have no face to show you. You left me to take care of your teenage sons. Believe me, I did keep my promise to you. They were brilliant at school. Both went to university with scholarships. I gave them all my love and they had everything money could buy. They seemed happy. I gave them enough freedom. They never gave me a reason to question them. My friends often wondered how I had managed to bring them up so well, single-handed. I was so proud! Yet... Somu missed something. I must have failed him in some way. Or else, he wouldn't have done such a thing.

Bharati, I used to think you were unlucky. You had missed all the fun, all the pride of seeing your sons reach the prime of their lives. But now I know why you have gone before me. A gentle soul like you, God wished to spare you from the agony. I was always proud of my judgements. Wasn't I? I had thought I was meting out justice to the wronged ones...Before I put my signature to one of those capital punishments, I used to spend sleepless nights thinking and rethinking, weighing the pros and cons. Yet that one signature of mine could have... must have harmed many lives! How many mothers, how many fathers, how many wives must have cursed me? Yes, I am convinced now. Or else, I wouldn't have had to face this ordeal, this anguish of seeing my own son at the end of a rope!

Bharati, you will be surprised to know what was the first thought that crossed my mind. I thought clinically, dispassionately, as I would at one of the criminal cases – the body had to be sent for post-mortem. And then a shooting pain went through my head. My son, mutilated, cut up and cobbled... No....I couldn't let that happen. Bharati, for the first time in my life, I thought of bribing. God is my witness. Our beautiful son sprawled at my feet. I thought, you wouldn't have forgiven me if I had allowed that. Poor Mukund, he managed everything. The suicide note left by Somu, and the rope, they said, were enough to prove that there was no foul play. Bharati, why did Somu do this to me? Where had I gone wrong? I must know. I have told Mukund to look into every sheet of paper in Somu's cupboard. Let him ransack Somu's room. But he must find out why Somu did such a thing...

Going through Somu's belongings was something

Mukund had been evading for the past one year. bookshelf had collected layers and layers of fine sooty dust. Mukund ran his eyes around the room. The walls were bare. The easels on which Somu had done his oil paintings– garish looking goddesses (Mukund used to tease him that they resembled popular film stars) and a few splashes of colour in glaring geometrical motifs, which he liked to call modern art, had all been taken down. Father had taken them to Delhi and had hung them in his room. For father, Somu was Piccaso and Leonardo da Vinci all rolled into one. Mukund had never seen his father so distraught. The authority, the confidence with which he used to go around – all gone. He refused to speak to the friends who called on him. Even to the servants, he mumbled as though he was afraid to speak to them. How could Mukund console his father when he himself felt so shattered? Somu, who was just a year younger than him, was not only his brother, but also his best friend and companion. Clearing the cobwebs, he walked around the room. When Somu and he were kids, when their mother was alive, he had shared this room with Somu. His cot faced the wall and Somu's had faced the window.

I used to wake up in the middle of the night and listen to Somu's singsong voice – Barah duni chaubees, Barah tiya

..ttees – chanting the multiplication tables tunefully. Sometimes, he would recite a poem that had perhaps been taught that day at school. He never got over the habit of talking in his sleep. When we were at the law school, the fiery arguments with which he argued his cases used to keep me awake all night. In fact, I didn't have to read books. I just had to listen to him in the nights to get through my exams.

Somu's sleepwalking was another big joke that went round our family circle. He would get up in the night, pick up his books, shove them into his bag and get out of the room. Mother or father, or one of the servants, would bring him back and quietly put him to bed. I still vividly remember the day when he got up from the bed and started running in the corridor. It was the month of Ashadh. The river in our village was in full spate. All evening, we boys swam from one end of the river to the other, or spent our time diving and taking dips. I went after him to bring him back to the room. Before I could catch him, he took a leap across the railings and went diving to the courtyard. But nothing happened to Somu. It was a miraculous escape. We brought him back to the bed all in one piece. But how mother wept that day! She took him to a doctor; but his medicines didn't work on him. Then she got a hakeem home, and it was his powders and pills that finally cured Somu of his sleepwalking.

Rows and rows of books. Mukund pulled them out

of the shelves. He threw open all the cupboards. The neatly stacked clothes, check and striped shirts, ties hung on a string on the inside part of the door. He felt as though he had come into the room to borrow a shirt from Somu. A whiff of Brute, Somu's favourite cologne, hit Mukund. He put his hands on his face and sank down on the floor. It wasn't going to be easy, going through Somu's belongings. But he had to do it. Father had asked him to do so.

Mukund dusted the books and piled them on the side. Somu never wrote diaries. He had often told him, diary writing was the hobby of sentimental women. Where could he look for clues? He was at a loss. On the lower shelf, Somu's sketchbooks had been neatly arranged. Somu was very fond of making sketches. You never knew when or how he would arrest you on the pages. Mukund idly flipped through the pages. His spirits lifted as he found himself drawn across the pages. Suited and booted, he was seated on a bench in the University Park. His slightly crooked nose had been made to look like a hook. And then he took note of his own expression: open-mouthed, he was staring at a pair of girls who were looking into the fishpond on the other end of the park. Mukund chuckled.

As far as I remember, I have never chased girls. Either I was too lazy or too shy. In fact, I usually stay away from girls. But it is quite amusing to learn how Somu had visualised me.

Another page, father in the court, sitting on the seat of the judge. The scar on his jaws has been given such a prominence that it looked as though he had a cleft chin.

Oh, my! What was he doing in the courtroom? He was puffing at a hookah! Father never smoked. What was Somu up to? I never knew he had a flair for cartoons! Mother's sketch was not a cartoon. She sat in front of the mirror, garlands on her hair, loaded with jewellery; but I had never seen her that way. I wish I had seen the sketches earlier. I wish I had asked Somu why he had sketched us in such a way, totally different from what we were. Did he enjoy seeing us that way?

Another sketchbook opened with the picture of a boy. He didn't resemble anyone Mukund knew. Ahead of him, there was a shadow, the boy's shadow; he seemed to be chasing his own shadow. Below the picture Somu had scribbled.

Dr. Jekyll had to down a concoction to become Hyde. I can do it so simply. See that shadow. I will give life to it.

Mukund turned the pages. Somu had made self-portraits. Whip in hands, he was chasing workers in a maze field. A beggar with a bowl, Somu was kicking him away. Mukund was puzzled. Art, he thought was the expression of one's genuine self. Somu was always kind to every one. Then why had he portrayed himself so differently? A little disturbed, he flipped the pages. Somu stared at him from every page— a lecherous smile, a frown, a sneer, and glaring eyes, eyes popping out in surprise, a face distorted by anger—so many faces of Somu! What did all this mean?

Nava rasa or a multifaced demon? Ha ha ha!!

Somu's caption intrigued Mukund. The next sketchbook was a mixture of landscape and portraits. There were no caricatures. Some of them were beautifully coloured. Mukund looked at the boys playing in the football ground. On the next page was an amusing picture. The ladies from the neighbourhood were busy squeezing mangoes and spreading the pulp on the mats. The bright sun was stationed right above their heads. Mukund looked for the scarecrow. Yes, it was there. When they were little boys, during the mango season, Somu and he used to help the ladies make mango papads. Somu would put up the funniest possible scarecrows for them. A big bowl full of fresh mango pulp, that was what they got as a reward for their labours. The good old days...

Yet another homely scene— a young girl was milking the cow, the white cow with black spots, which gave the maximum milk for the house. The girl looked familiar.

Where had he seen her? The next page, and the next page, the same girl in different poses. Yes... now he could recognise her. For sure, it was the youngest daughter of their cook. Gathering together the pallav of her sari, which had slipped off her shoulders, her luscious youthful figure delicately outlined, she looked like a seductress. There were a few more pictures— another girl, a little short and stout, but attractive, standing with books in hand, in front of a school building. Mukund was sure, he had never seen this girl.

And he saw the scrawl. Wasn't it a nursery rhyme?

Georgy Porgy pudding and pie,
Kissed the girls and made them cry.
When the girls began to smile,
Georgy Porgy ran away.

The next picture was absolutely out of this world.

Three golden deer in a lush green grove. They seemed to be on a run. The one with the three-pronged antlers running ahead of the other two, seemed to be the stag. The two behind him, slightly smaller in size, looked like females.

They trail me as though I am a musk deer
But where are the musk-pods?
Where is the musk?

The lines Somu had scribbled under them, were they from a poem? Mukund couldn't place them. He had never been a voracious reader like Somu.

Mukund went back to the portraits of the young women. Would they know something about his brother, something that he himself did not know? The thought made him feel a trifle sad. But he couldn't, and he shouldn't, rule out any possibilities. He didn't want to go hunting down people like a detective. But father had sent him here to find the rationale of his brother's death.

Finding the cook's house was not a problem. Ever since father left, the house had been shut down. The cook, who had nothing to do, usually spent his afternoons playing cards or gossiping with the unemployed men of the neighbourhood. As Mukund entered the house two children, came out. They could hardly believe it was the young master who had come to call on them. They looked at him in awe and one of the boys nervously muttered.

'Father is not at home.'

'Where is your sister?'

They looked at him blankly.

'Where is Kammo? Is she not your sister?'

Mukund saw a movement near the door. Kammo stood in the doorway, with downcast eyes, her head discreetly covered with the loose end of her sari.

'You come to our house often. Don't you?'

There was no answer.

'You milk the cows. Right?'

She nodded.

'What other work do you do in the house?'

'I help my father in the kitchen,'she said softly.

'You knew my brother well. Didn't you?'Mukund's question, so abruptly flung at her, must have caught her by surprise. She shook her head, a vehement no. Mukund's next move totally unarmed her. He flipped open the sketch books and pushed it under her nose.'Here, is that not you?'

The girl trembled like a leaf and collapsed at

Mukund's feet.'Had I known he would do such a thing, I wouldn't have told him that... 'she blurted out between sobs.

'What did you tell him?' Mukund's voice was like a whip.

'Oh! I told him I was carrying.' She was weeping uncontrollably.

'Where is the child?'

'There was no child. I thought I would scare him. He might even consent to marry me!'

Mukund stared at her in stunned silence. It took him some time to figure out the import of her words. Then he pushed the portrait of the other woman towards her.

'Do you recognise this woman?' Mukund could trace a flash of anger in Kammo's eyes.

'Yes, I have seen her. She is the teacher at the government school. Two years ago, she came to the village.'

It took a couple of days to track down the teacher. She lived at the river end of the village with her old ailing father. The teacher vehemently denied she had ever known Somu. Mukund quietly put forward the sketchbook. Her defiant, level eyes were immediately lowered.

'Yes, he was my friend,' she whispered almost inaudibly.

'Only a friend, or much more than that? How often did you see him?'

'He used to visit me on weekends.'

'When did you last see him?'

Her face was death-pale. Her eyes glinted in an unnatural way. She pursed her lips together as though she would seal them.

'You must tell me all about it. I must know. I am his brother.' Mukund reasoned with her.

'I would rather not speak.'

'In that case, I may have to summon you to the court.' Mukund now had to resort to threats.

She shrank to the corner of the sofa, covered her face with both her hands and spoke softly not to Mukund but to herself.

'He never talked about marriage. Whenever I broached the subject, he would laugh it off. So I told him I was carrying...'

'Where is your baby?'Mukund couldn't help intervening.

'Baby? The baby was a myth... I thought that would make him own me...'

'When did you tell him this?'Mukund asked her in

a shaky voice.

'The day before his death. Yes... I have sent him to his death. You must punish me for it. Take me to the court. I will confess...'

Blinded by tears of sorrow or shame or anger, Mukund didn't quite know, he groped his way out of the house, leaving the woman behind to rave and rant.

When Anand's car came screeching down the gravelled path and pulled into the driveway, Mukund was pacing up and down in the garden. He had completely forgotten about Anand. His cousin Anand was a doctor who had a flourishing practice in the city. He had promised Mukund, he would drive down to the village for the weekend. The idea of spending days and nights in an abandoned house, even though it was his own dear home, had initially scared him and he had requested Anand to take a few days off and join him.

It was a great relief to have Anand around. Across the dinner table, Mukund narrated the harrowing tale of his scouting. The sordid shameful story, he had stumbled on. Anand choked on a fish bone that he had swallowed in haste. Mukund made a huge round ball of rice and pushed it down Anand's throat. 'Come on. Gulp it down in one single breath,' Mukund ordered affectionately. Mother used to do that whenever Somu or he had swallowed a fish bone. Anand chased the ball of rice with a glass full of chilled water and cleared his throat.

'What did you say, Mukund. Somu ruined two women? Impossible! Let me tell you a secret, a professional secret. I would have never divulged it had you not told me this. Do you know why Somu gave up his job in the city and joined uncle here? He had come once to the hospital to see me. People were standing in a queue, waiting for a potency test. Somu jokingly said, 'Let me also test'. When the results came, I had no heart to tell him the truth. But he insisted on knowing it. So I told him he couldn't ever father a child for any woman, Mukund.'

Mukund felt dazed. Somu was not capable of fathering a child and he knew it! What did that mean? He knew the two women were lying to him? He could have exposed them any day. Then, why should Somu end his life? Mukund turned to his cousin.

'They loved him so desperately that they didn't mind telling such a big lie to stake their claim on him. That is frightening! Such a demanding love... May be...'

May be, may be! Mukund was not convinced. He wrung his hands in exasperation.

They trail me down as though I am a musk deer
But where are the musk pods?
Where is the musk?

Once again, the lines came back to haunt him. His father was anxiously waiting for him to bring some news. What could he tell him? How could he comfort his poor father? Should he tell him, he had found no clues?

Mahadev's Garden

Mahadev's garden was the talk of the town. He didn't own acres of land. Nor did he possess anything like a riverfront villa to plan and experiment landscaping or cascading. A man of moderate means, not brilliant, not even ambitious, he managed to emerge out of college, a graduate. It was an achievement in itself. He took up the first job that came his way, as an accountant in one of the local medical firms. Of course, he knew how to make the best of what he had. He worked hard, cultivated the right kind of people and soon rose to the rank of an officer.

His wife Radha Bai brought with her a modest dowry. A down to earth man, he invested it in a cottage left behind by a family that had migrated to the U.S. People laughed at him for buying a house in such a dilapidated state. But the price was affordable. In fact, it was so temptingly low that Mahadev just grabbed it. He was confident he could transform the ruined cottage into a beauty, which he did in no time. He did not go looking for architects. With the help of a few labourers he pulled down windows and doors, changed the entrance, repaired the leaking roof, plastered and painted the walls and planned and lay, around the house, a neat little garden. The garden, a semicircle in shape, set the house idyllically, in a leafy frame. Mahadev had worked a miracle on the house. To those who walked on the road, the cottage appeared like a house in a picture postcard.

The wicket gate, which had an arch-shaped arbour of creamy cherry blossoms, opened to a narrow pathway, fringed on either side by ferns. The path led to a flight of stone steps straight to the main entrance. Mahadev did not believe in identifying his house by a number, as the City Corporation decreed. He chose a name for it. *Aishwarya.* Yes, that was what he would call his home. Prosperity for himself, his wife and his little daughter. In golden letters, he inscribed the name *Aishwarya* on the right side, above the panelled door.

The layout of Mahadev's garden could have been the envy of any horticulturist. With great care and precision, he fenced the garden, not with barbed wires, but with tough thorny shrubs sporting flowers, which gave out a strong pungent smell. It helped to keep cattle away. In the four corners of the garden, he planted varieties of palm under which he grew colourful beds of begonias and violets. He chose flowers and foliages, perennials and annuals of various shapes and colours. He mixed and matched, blended and contrasted and the result was a riot of colours and a range of intriguing shapes. It was a small, but breathtakingly beautiful garden. As seeds sprouted into shoots, and spread into stems to branch off, budding and blooming, Mahadev stood watching as though mesmerised.

Radha, his wife, was slender and small-made. Her *startled deer* eyes, which made her look so lost and loveable, were hauntingly beautiful. Of course, Mahadev doted on her. But she dressed so sloppily. The colours she chose! How could she be so clumsy? As for the art of housekeeping, she knew nothing at all. Mahadev was quite shocked. He couldn't blame her though. After all she was a farmer's daughter. Sure, she felt uprooted in the big city and Mahadev's urbanity must have been unnerving. In any case, he couldn't expect her to be an architect or an artist like him. Mahadev knew he must take charge of the situation at once. He happily set about arranging the wardrobe of his wife. He made sure he picked the right colours and the right design—pastel shades and small flowery prints. And Radha soon emerged as a worthy match for her husband. After all, wasn't Mahadev an immaculately dressed man? The creases of his trousers were always intact. He wore shirts, only white, which were spotlessly clean. His tie was perfectly knotted, and his black leather shoes were polished to shine.

During the early years of their marriage, Radha's effusive ways—Mahadev called her naïve and artless—used to embarrass him. It might be morning or evening. Radha might have been in the kitchen, frying fish. Or, she could have been drying her hair over the fumes of incense sticks. If an aircraft came zooming by, ladle in hand, towel flung over the shoulder, she would rush out of the house. Straining her neck, with wonder-struck eyes she would follow the flight of *the giant silver bird*. That's what she called it. "Those tiny dots, are they not the windows of the plane? Can you look down through those windows? I am sure, your head would go spinning," she would gush on breathlessly. When she walked on the streets with her husband, an ice-cream parlour, the brilliantly lit display-window of a shop, even a tall building - anything and everything, could make her swoon. Credit should go to Mahadev. He never lost patience with his wife. Neither did he ever bully her. Stern looks, stony silences, or a few frowns were more than enough to bring her on line.

Radha had no great talent to boast of. But she had a sweet voice and she could copy the catchy tunes of the popular movies almost effortlessly. But Mahadev had his own views about music. 'There is nothing great about vocal music,' he often told her. 'Why don't you try to master an instrument? Give voice to a violin or a veena. You will know how much talent you have, how much power you have.'

Mahadev's wisdom always inspired her. She did get herself a veena. Turning the knobs on its sides, she tried to tighten and loosen the strings, moving her fingers up and down with devotion. But, as luck would have it, the veena refused to respond to her. That was how her foray into the world of music had come to a full stop.

When the little girl arrived, Radha was only too happy to leave her in the safe hands of her husband. Mahadev took all decisions and masterfully managed all crises. She cooked and cleaned, washed and bathed Pushpa and dressed her, always, in white muslin frocks, as her husband had wished. With the precision of a wound clock, she measured her days by the errands she ran for the family.

Radha would have loved to cuddle and croon over her little daughter. But she knew it wouldn't be proper. Mahadev wouldn't have approved. After all, he had high hopes for his daughter. He wanted her to flower into a fine lady. No parent was as enthusiastic as Mahadev. At least that was what Pushpa's teachers thought. He supervised her schoolwork, helped her with all her assignments. There was no question of Radha coping with all that. Numbers puzzled her - she kept a neat record of accounts at home though! History and geography, she had left far behind. In any case, she was awfully busy. When she was not cooking, she was stitching. When she was not stitching, she was cleaning.

But father was always there for Pushpa. Mahadev taught her how to play badminton and chess. He sent her across to the old Anglo- Indian lady who lived all by herself in the corner house, to learn piano and painting. It was Mahadev again who told her to graduate in Home Science. Pushpa had always wished to be a doctor. She was disappointed. It was one of the rare occasions when she had tried to talk to her mother. Pushpa distinctly remembered what her mother had said, 'Father knows best.'

Years ago, she remembered when she had sketched a garden spider in her drawing book, her father had been visibly disturbed. He had asked Pushpa to sit in the garden and draw whatever she liked best. Of course, he had expected her to turn up with the reproduction of a rose or a sunflower. But the eight gnarled legs of the spider, and its silvery web, mystified Pushpa and she had copied them on the paper.

'A delicate girl like you, how could you choose a spider?' Father had been astonished.

'What is so delicate about being a girl? What is wrong in sketching a spider?'

She had turned to her mother. Mother had said quietly, 'Father knows best.'

When Radha grew weak and pale, Mahadev was quite concerned. The family doctor ruled out any major illness. She needed nutritious food, rest, fresh air and some tonics. That was what he had recommended. But strangely enough, Radha only grew weaker and paler. Her movements were no longer lithe and graceful. With stooping shoulders and downcast eyes, she moved around the house trying to cope with the chores. Inexplicably, no specialist could explain why her skin reacted so strongly to the rays of the sun. If she ventured out even for a short while, her skin would weep and erupt into small angry red pimples. Gradually, she stopped moving out of the house. Shielding herself from the glare of the sun, in rooms darkened by thick curtains, she spent her last days bent over her prayer books. When she died, the doctor said her death was due to heart failure. How strange! Neither Mahadev nor Pushpa ever suspected she had a weak heart.

Mahadev spent almost a week, scanning the family album carefully. At last he pulled out, what he thought, was the best photograph of his wife– Radha in her bridal finery. He was about to fix the photo into an old frame. But Pushpa, for once, put her foot down. It was a black and white photograph, frayed and yellowed at the corners. She insisted on getting it coloured and enlarged, whatever the charges might be. It was worthwhile. All her troubles. The photographer seemed to have put his entire technical skill into it–mounting, laminating, and adding all sorts of special effects to turn it into a soulful portrait. And there she was, so frail, so ethereal like an angel– a guardian angel, perched on the wall, keeping a fond watch over the family.

The day mother died was painfully alive in Pushpa's mind. It was a winter afternoon, a Sunday. She was in the study room, grappling with an equation in algebra. A fresh fruity flavour wafted to her nostrils. A date cake! Pushpa's favourite. But mother was so sick she shouldn't have been anywhere near the kitchen. Pushpa ran out of the room. Radha had just taken the cake out of the oven. On the kitchen floor, soaked in sweat, she had soon collapsed. Pushpa had no appetite for food for days. But she had guarded the date cake furiously for one full week, refusing to share it with anyone.

Somehow, retirement didn't bother Mahadev. Friends had their own fears. Radha gone, Pushpa grown up and busy with her studies, home couldn't have had much charm for him. But it was heartening to see Mahadev back in the garden with renewed vigour. Weeding out flowerbeds, mowing the lawn, repairing the fence, he spent his days blissfully!

That was the time when he had turned to bonsai. To begin with, it looked like a passing fancy. Soon, it became a passion with him. For days and days, he combed the market and came home with containers and pots of variegated shapes and sizes - round, rectangular, oval and square. In no time, he mastered the art and science of bonsai. Methodically, like a scientist, he measured the soil, sieved and dried it, planted seedlings strategically in the containers— in the middle, to the right or to the left according to the shapes he had envisaged and planned for them. He acquired a brand new pruning kit for himself. It was a treat to watch him at work. With great care, he cut the root ends. Delicately, neatly, he pinched and pruned the stems. With skilled fingers and appropriate tools, he gave the trunks an intriguing twist, a shapely slant. If the branches took off on their own in an attempt to rise and spread, he arrested them promptly and expertly with a wire or a twine. Not only peepals and pines, Mahadev successfully managed to dwarf even fruit trees - orange, apple and lemon. The miniatures stood on attractive stands or on raised platforms as the crowning glory of his garden.

Mahadev had always wished Pushpa would lend him a hand in the garden! Weeding, watering or at least cleaning. She could have. In fact, she should have definitely done her bit. But he was surprised, even hurt, that she had never offered him any help. Only the other night, across the dinner table, Mahadev had tried his best to draw her out.

"Pushpa, have you seen my latest bonsai? This time I want to experiment with pomegranate. The branches are already shaping."

For a moment, Pushpa stared at him in a strange way and had gone back moodily to her aloo bhaji and bhath. She was being difficult. Or distant? Mahadev was unnecessarily getting worried. She was a bit tense, preoccupied. Naturally, with examinations round the corner. But his daughter wasn't quite herself, Mahadev was sure. Something was weighing on her mind. She was too silent! She had never been a chatterbox. But now, she hardly talked. Why had she become so unpredictable? Last week, when she returned from her college picnic, she had almost made a scene. All because Mahadev had chaperoned her to the picnic spot and back home. Once she joined her friends, he had left for the public library nearby. Sure, in the evening he had gone back to fetch her home. Imagine Pushpa bursting into tears and accusing him that he had humiliated her! Today, when Pushpa said she was going to attend the wedding of one of her close friends, he hadn't insisted on accompanying her. But the house was only a few streets away. It was already evening. Pushpa should be home any moment. Mahadev moved to the garden. The orange tree, he remembered, needed some trimming.

Whatever had happened to the pomegranate buds? A brilliant red, anxious to bloom, there had been five of them he remembered. He had counted only this morning! Where were they? The rectangular tray, in which the orange tree stood, had a crack right at in the middle. What a calamity! One of the prized branches of the pine tree had snapped. The missing limb lay a few yards away. Mahadev ran to the fence. Was there any gap in the fence? The Dalmatian next door? Had he broken out of his leash and crashed into his garden? He looked around in alarm. The lemon tree—only the stump remained! All the branches had been cut off. Yes, they had been neatly cut off.... No Dalmatian could have done that...

The wicket gate clicked open. It was Meenu, Pushpa's friend. In her usual busy way, she breezed in. Behind her, the dainty gate swung to and fro on its delicate hinges. She had not bothered to close it, Mahadev noted, with a frown. Careless and clumsy! How could Pushpa be so friendly with her? But where was Pushpa?

'I left Pushpa at the station. She is taking the Frontier Mail to Bombay.' Bombay? 'Come on, Uncle! Don't tell me you didn't know. She has got a teaching job in Bombay. Lucky, it is a residential school. Don't worry. She will be fine. Here, she has left a note for you and the keys.'

That was the duplicate set of house keys which Pushpa used to keep with herself. Mahadev stared at the note blankly. On a piece of crumpled paper, she had scribbled, 'I am going away.'

Going away? Why? She never said she had any such plan! Has she really gone to Bombay? Where could she have gone? Mahadev slowly walked towards the splintered base of the pine. He must file it. At once. He opened the pruning kit. Clippers and scissors, trowels and shears, one after the other, everything tumbled out. Kneeling on the hard earth with shaking hands, hands neatly covered in garden - gloves, he rummaged for the right tool listlessly. His gold-rimmed spectacles sat delicately balanced on the bridge of his aquiline nose. The cool evening breeze fanned the leaves and shook the ripening oranges. Mahadev shivered slightly.

The Thirteenth Day

Outside the headmaster's room, on the left corner of the long corridor, hung the round disc-like metal gong. The four o' clock sun, in a generous mood, had lent a glow to it. The bell now looked burnished, almost new. Above the pillared column of the weather-beaten school building, on a narrow wooden ledge, rested the hammer. Each time Ummar Ikka came out of the office room— the glint of the live beedi held tightly between the lips, gave him a look of added importance—and took the hammer down to hit the metal gong, the children beamed. Ummar Ikka spoke to the children through the language of the bell. With years of practice he had evolved an inimitable style, uniquely his. A single sharp knock meant moving on to the next period; three long dragging knocks were for the morning assembly and the three mighty bangs followed by a soft rhythmic pounding which trailed off to a dying fall - the most melodious one for the kids — were for the end of the day.

Shoving books, lunchbox, pencils and all those weird items picked up from the school compound or from the neighbour's desk into their bags, the kids burst out of their boring classrooms, shouting and yelling, singing and laughing, pushing and fighting with each other. The headmaster and even his deadly rattan failed to intimidate them at this hour of the day. Shreya and Soumya, the twin sisters were already past the door. Looking over their shoulder impatiently, they called out to Karthi to hurry up. The three of them usually walked together – a distance of one and a half kilometres – back to their house, towards the south end of the beach road. Karthi gathered her belongings unenthusiastically, shook the dust off her skirt and dragged her feet towards the door.

'Is your cousin, still with you?'

'And your uncle?'

'Aren't you proud you have such a famous uncle?'

When uncle came to the school for the annual day people stood on either side of the road to cheer him. And all the while, he stood in the open jeep with folded hands, his chin burrowed in garlands.

'Your uncle, you remember, threw the rose garland and the bouquet to the crowd. My brother was so lucky he caught it. He has kept them pressed against cellophane sheets. All shrivelled and dried up now. But he has carefully put them away on the top shelf of the cupboard. Has your cousin brought sport shoes for you?'

'No...not this time.'

Uncle gave away the prizes on the annual day. Karthi

had won two medals for the obstacle race and long jump. As she walked back to her seat with a spring in her step and a proud smile on her lips, Devu had stared at her long legs and giggled. Her dusty feet clumsily clad in frayed Hawaii slippers obviously looked funny and disgusting to her city cousin.

'Do you really run without shoes?'

Karthi wished her cousin didn't have such a loud voice. In any case, the girls were straining their ears to catch every word uttered by the daughter of their chief guest! Why did Devu have to come to the school? But of course, uncle took her wherever he went. The pink silk skirt and the butterfly bow on her hair really suited her. She looked a fairy. Karthi looked down at her blue uniform skirt and the white greying blouse. The medal and the certificate were forgotten. She didn't know how, when or why, but the spell had snapped. She straightened her shoulders. And casually, almost defiantly, she said to herself, 'I feel so free... it is so much easier, without shoes. I could fly on my naked feet and win races if I wished.'

Devu had been sympathetic though. She had promised Karthi a pair of brand new sports shoes next time she came. But that was two years ago, the time when Devu and she were friends. She had to be good to Karthi. Who else would have taken her around their sprawling land, to every nook and corner of the three-acre compound around the house, beyond the serpent grove, to the forbidden territory of the western pond where Muthashi's younger sister had fallen in a fit of epilepsy and drowned. The stone steps running down to the mossy green pond had long since crumbled to a few scattered crevices. But while spreading net for fish, the workers had cut steps all around the mud bank. Skipping on those steps was dangerous, but fun. She could spend hours looking at the tortoise and the snail cruising on the slope, as though scheduled for a serious meeting! The blue and gold kingfisher, diving in and out of the pond each time with fresh prey.

When she took Devu to her favourite haunt, Devu had clapped her hands and laughed in wonder. Karthi wouldn't have normally shared her private zoo cum bird sanctuary with anyone. Devu knew she was being honoured. Karthi had to put her foot down though, when Devu leaned down to reach the floating water lilies. Who knew, a water snake might surface, and her city cousin might faint. To Devu, every wild bush and flower around was a source of wonder. The white spittoon flowers, the knuckle knots—Karthi had showed her how to burst them open with just the right pressure. She was very amused when Devu started chanting the names of every plant and flower, as though she wished to memorise them! She wanted to eat nothing but the blood-red berries and the sour star fruits that were specially plucked for her. Naturally, that summer, she had simply clung to Karthi.

But this time, Devu was so different. Was it because of the Dubai auntie? Auntie had brought a bag full of gifts for Devu. So many games: a brand new cassette player and the *Ruby cube*! Why wouldn't she share any of the games with Karthi? Had she forgotten all the gifts she had given her last time? When no one was around, Karthi had taken the cube in her hands and spun it around, blue, green and yellow, like a rainbow in shreds. With her nimble fingers, in minutes she had set it in pattern. And imagine Devu had spent hours struggling to set it!

Devu looked grown up too... She had shining painted nails, shaped like crescent moons. And she was so conscious about her frocks and skirts!

'Look at Devika, she is no longer a child. And our Karthi! Younger only by a year, still flat-chested!' Karthi had heard the milkmaid whispering to mother.

'Devika is a city girl. Why are you surprised? City girls, you know, grow fast.' Running her hands through Karthi's long curly hair, Mother had just smiled.

Last evening, when she peeped into Balu's room, the cassette player was screaming some crazy music. And Balu and Devu were dancing, throwing their arms and feet around. Was it a drill or a parade? Looking at them was enough to make her head go spinning! Every time she tried to join them why did they have to shoo her away? Uncle and aunties too would have nothing to do with her. They were so busy inspecting every room, even the cellars and the lofts. Last night, they had locked themselves in Muthashi's room. Through the window, Karthi had seen how they were pulling out papers, reading, writing, counting and arguing! Devu's mother with the round spectacles perched on her nose, looked like one of the witches Karthi had seen on the pages of Amar Chitrakatha. They looked so serious. Like an army united, ready to strike, bent on waging a war. But against whom? Karthi wondered why her father and mother were keeping themselves away.

'Who is this? Karthika Kutti? Why did you come to school today? Tomorrow is the Thirteenth Day celebration, isn't it? You have left all the guests at home?' She turned back. It was Ummar Ikka. His umbrella tickled her on the neck. 'Finally, Muthashi is gone. How long she had resisted death! Your mother, poor thing, is free at last. Massaging, bathing and cleaning - years of slaving. And after all that, the old woman wouldn't even look at her... Tell your father I will be there in the evening. I will supervise the pandals and arrange for the cauldrons and firewood. After all, it is the funeral festivity of our Mantri's mother. I expect no less than two hundred guests.'

Karthi walked on. But the thought kept nagging her. Why should there be pandals and a feast at death? Of course, Ummar Ikka would be of great help to Father. After school hours, Ummar Ikka often came home either to arrange for the sale of coconuts and chicken eggs, or for clearing the orchards. Father limped around all day. But in such a big estate, how much can a lame man do? Whenever Ummar Ikka went to the city, he brought Father tobacco and bottles of medicine. He would sit with father in the backyard and chat for long hours. Mother always frowned at the long evenings he spent with Ummar Ikka.

But the next morning, Karthi found Father in a playful mood. He would offer to make toys for Karthi. His long fingers, pale and delicately tapering, worked skilfully, nimbly on ola, the dried palm leaves or on a vazhapola, the fresh peels of the banana bark. Within minutes, he would shape tiny utensils, or a doll, or even a ball to bounce around and play with, for her. He would pick a few sticks and the tiny kochanga, the baby coconuts fallen from the coconut tree and like a magician, transform them into chariots and carts. If only he could breathe life into them, Karthi often wished, she could wheel away to a fairy land!

Whenever uncle came on a visit, Karthi wondered why father grew quiet and moody. Uncle would sit with him late into nights, tallying records and receipts. Karthi could not understand why uncle always shouted at her father. Muthashi didn't spare him either. Even Dubai auntie teased him all the time. If his left leg had become lifeless and dysfunctional, it was not his fault.

When Pavati swept the orchard she always kept the other workers entertained. Her anecdotes— she had a bag full of them—were hilarious. Of course, all her stories were centred on the family members. After all she, as the oldest servant in the house, knew all the secrets of the family. Karthi had heard her confiding to the fellow workers, 'Our young master, you know, was not born lame. It was the mistake of the midwife. What a difficult childbirth it was! She kept pulling and pulling at the baby's legs, to bring it out of the womb somehow. Thank God, only one leg was harmed. At least he can hop around.'

'But why does the old lady hate her own son?'

'Oh! That is a long story. The Mantri master was her favourite, even as a child. He was brainy, straight shouldered and handsome. But I know how he used to treat his younger brother.... When his friends came home, he would make the little boy grovel before them and have a good laugh. What tales he used to carry to his mother! He made sure the poor boy got thrashed and punished for no fault of his. Ugly and dim-witted, his mother never missed a chance to remind him of that. But for the old master, he wouldn't have even seen the gates of the school. It was a few years after the death of the old master. The elder one was already out somewhere, in a big position. The younger one was at home, taking care of the land. During the rainy season he fell ill. What an attack of typhoid it was! The girl took such good care of him. Staying awake all night, mopping his forehead, giving him medicines and food. Naturally, the young man fell for her. When he recovered, he married her. The old woman could never accept it. Pappi Amma was an orphan left in the care of the old master. (Why did they call her Pappi

Amma? Karthi wondered. Father always called her mother Padmini. And it sounded so sweet) Pappi's mother was one of the maids in the house. But no one knew who her father was! The old woman never forgave her son for marrying beneath their caste. And as for the daughter-in-law, to her dying day, she had refused to speak to her. Kind or harsh, not even a word passed between them all these years...'

Karthi knew too well, Pavati was not making up a story. She had never heard Muthashi call her mother by her name. 'Karthi! Karthi!' Muthashi always called for her. It didn't matter whether she was at home or not. Mother knew it was she who was being summoned. Squatting on the floor in front of the banana leaf, she would speak in an aerial voice.

'Papadam man has wound up his business or what? All the pickle jars seem to be empty.' Mother would immediately come out of the kitchen with papadam or pickle.

Ummar Ikka was right. By the time Karthi reached home, preparations for the funeral feast were in full swing. Workers were running around carrying rice bags, head-loads of vegetables and firewood. Women were sitting in the courtyard, chopping heaps of yam and gourd. Uncle was having some serious discussion with the brahmanan, the priest of the temple nearby. Many people were waiting for their turn to have a word with uncle.

Dawn broke with hectic activity. Karthi sniffed at the air, taking in all the flavours and fragrance wafting around. The sweet smell of the smoking homemade coconut oil. The crisp golden banana chips! She ran around the pandals and stood staring at those sweaty men perched on rickety stools, stirring rice and milk in huge cauldrons over the naked fire. She watched with fascination, the damask-white concoction of milk and rice--- foaming and surfing over the rims. Beggars, cripples and the blind, had all lined up on the narrow road in front of the house. Pavati said they would all be given food and clothes and they would go home blessing Muthashi. Will they really bless Muthashi? When beggars turned up at the gate on Saturdays, Muthashi used to curse them. It was mother who used to feed them—at times on the sly.

Karthi had never, in the eleven years of her young life, seen anything like these rituals. There were three Brahmin priests. The senior priest, pot-bellied and gap-toothed, sat in the middle, flanked by the younger ones, pale-complexioned with clean-shaven eggheads. On the tortoise-shaped planks they sat importantly, chanting mantras. Off and on, through the darbha rings they wore on their forefingers, they kept sprinkling water on the family members. The way they twisted and turned their hands, they looked like kathakali masters. Karthi controlled her giggles with great difficulty. Devu and Balu were also giggling. They were sitting next to uncle.

My God! Look at the thing shining around Devu's neck? Wasn't it the Pavan Mala of Muthashi? How Karthi loved it! Every year on Vishu morning, Muthashi used to place it in her hands generously and would then sternly order her to give it back. Straight from bed, rubbing her sleepy eyes, she sat before the Vishu kani and looked at those glittering sovereigns strung together in a gold chain. They appeared to her like beacons of light. Being the only girl child at home, Muthashi was simply, symbolically following a custom. Everyone knew the Pavan Mala was not being gifted to Karthi. Yet one Vishu morning, Karthi had held on to the Mala and Muthashi had flown into a temper. Mother had forced open Karthi's tightly closed fists and had handed over Muthashi's property back to her. What was Devu doing with Muthashi's Pavan Mala?

'But she could have left something for Karthi... At

least a pinch of gold for her ears! And my daughter doted on the Pavan Mala... You remember, last Vishu...' Mother was sobbing...

'You are worried about gold? Our Karthi is a gem by herself - She needs no gold. What if they sell the estate? Where will we be?' Something seemed to have caught at Father's throat.

Karthi watched the priests getting up from their seats. The senior priest rolled a leaf full of rice into a cone. Yam and gourd, pepper and sesame seeds sat on it, making black and white festoons around it. Balancing the mound of rice on a banana leaf, he carried it to the southern part of the courtyard. The crowd was at his heel. The old man squinted against the afternoon sky and looked up and down as though searching for someone. He dipped his hands in water and brought his palms together. The younger priests also joined. Clap ...clap, clap...Yes, they clapped louder and louder in chorus. Where were the crows? Were they not keen to fall on Muthashi's shradham feast?

Look at the huge dark clouds spinning across the southern end of the sky! Only a while ago the sun was brilliant! A sharp shower had already set in. The priests scrambled back to the safety of the corridor. The rain now came roaring down. Karthi watched the mound of rice first flattening and then running down the slope in rivulets. She looked around frantically. There it was—the umbrella. Behind the massive wooden door, which opened to Muthashi's room. Plucking it off the hook, she ran out into the rain. People looked at her in amazement. With an eerie feeling they watched the scene. Karthi was struggling to save the mound of rice. The umbrella could hardly shield it. Stretching her hands out, she tried again and again to gather the rice. 'The crows must eat the rice. Or else, as Pavati says, Muthashi will not go to heaven. Yes, the crows must eat the rice,' Karthi kept muttering to herself. Muthashi must go to heaven or else....

Pursuit

Sameera threw her head back and with a critical eye watched the image in the mirror. Youthful eyes- wide and liquid black- stared back at her. She pinched her face here and there. A suggestion of a shadow under the eyes? Dark circles? A few age-spots near the temples? With deft fingers, she mixed colours and dabbed them on the hollow of her cheeks, on the temples and the chin. She swept the brush, feather-like, on her face in skilful strokes, upward and downward, inward and outward. Silky soft shades of peach and melon blended in, and soon the sand-beige of her natural pallor deepened into a rich seductive honey-beige. Sameera really knew how to accentuate her assets and camouflage her blemishes. Her shimmering face emerged in the cloudy mirror like a full-blown flower coming out of the morning mist.

'Sameera, what a lovely case! Is it leather?' Meera exclaimed as she sleepwalked into the house after a gruelling day in the office.

'My foot! Leather indeed! Can't you see it is made of glossy rexene?'Chandu shouted from the terrace where he was grappling with his weights. 'Meera didi, it is Sameera's tool box. How naïve you are!' Admiring the rippling muscles of his arms, Chandu leaned on the railings to educate his elder sister.

'So many brushes, combs and paints. What is all this for?' Poor Meera! To her, whatever Sameera did was a source of wonder.

'Meera didi, have you never seen a make-up kit?' Sameera snapped.

'It must have cost you a fortune. Where did you get the money?'

'Why, am I not earning?'

'I earn three times more than you do. But Ma says it is not enough even to meet the grocery bills. How come you are left scot-free?'

'Why don't you keep some money away for yourself?'

'How can I? Ma knows the break-up of my allowances. She even remembers the dates when my increments are due,' Meera whined.

For the last ten years, Meera had been the bread-earner of the family. Father's meagre pension was just a drop in the ocean. Sameera was now a graduate and had found a teaching job for herself. But Chandu was in medical college and needed help. After the stroke he had suffered last year, father was almost confined to bed. Mornings and evenings, he would wheel himself out into the garden. He sat in his wheelchair, facing the gate, looking longingly at the speeding vehicles, at the formally dressed men and women hurrying to their workplaces, or at the school children, chaperoned by their mothers, skipping and running on the sidewalks.

Sliding on the balustrade, Chandu came crashing down on the floor and landed at Sameera's feet.

'Mirror, mirror, who is the fairest? Sameera, Sameera....' He circled around her with a war cry. 'But, tell me Sameera, how will you repair your squint?'

'Will you leave the poor girl in peace? Why? She has no squint. Her left eye is slightly smaller than her right eye. But that is for luck.' Sameera was really her mother's favourite. 'Sameera, you are again off for a wedding? Last month you had attended four weddings!'

'Oh Ma, why do you worry? I assure you, I only go for the marriages of my close friends.'

'Let the poor girl attend the weddings of her friends at least. No chance of a wedding in the family,' Father grumbled from the wheelchair.

'Don't you say such inauspicious things,' Mother flashed her angry eyes at father.

While the family buzzed around her, Sameera sat like a queen, unperturbed. She piled her hair up on the crown and carefully pinned it into a beehive puff.

She deposited the gift packet, colourfully wrapped and neatly tied with a tinsel bow, safely into her handbag. Trailing whiffs of French perfume, recently purchased at the flea market, Sameera glided out of the gate.

The wedding ceremony would start only at seven o'clock, that too, if the baraat reached on time! She had ample time. She could afford to wait for a bus. The bus stop was quite crowded. As she smoothened her hair and patted the puffs into place, she caught sight of the man. He was a tall and well-built young man. The thin carefully trimmed moustache stood out prominently against the healthy glow of his face. He stood, leaning on his motorbike, a few yards away from the bus stop. Sameera knew he was looking at her. Was there a smile on his face? Did she know him? No.... He was a total stranger. In a bit of a flurry, she turned her eyes to the jostling crowd that was trying to push its way into an overloaded bus. Why not take a cab? She could ensure that her dress and her makeup were intact. She hailed a passing cab and as she heaved herself into the seat, she heard the motorbike roaring into life. From the rear window, she had a glimpse of the man. He was riding close to the car. Could be a coincidence. He might be going in the same direction.

Sameera dismissed him from her mind.

The bride was an old friend of hers. The bridegroom was a doctor, settled in the U.S. Soon her friend would be flying away to New York. How exciting! Sameera sighed. She had not even seen the other big cities of India. The cab stopped near the festooned gate, which was decorated with marigolds and the auspicious leaves of the mango tree. The shrubs, which lined the adjoining garden, were blinking with multicoloured bulbs. She joined the young girls who sat in a circle around the bride. In shimmering silks, loaded with diamonds and gold, the bride looked charming and impressive.

'I am going to hide the groom's shoes and demand a big ransom,' one of the girls warned the coy bride.

'I won't let him cross the threshold unless he gives me a gold ring,' another threatened.

Along with the other girls, Sameera gently led the bashful bride to the mandap where the bridegroom was already seated. She stood a little away and watched the rituals intently. The smoke, which came curling up from the havan, made the scene a little cloudy. As the couple was completing their seventh round around the sacred fire, as Sameera along with others was showering rose petals on them, the face appeared on the opposite side. Yes, the young man on the motorbike was standing among the guests and he was winking at Sameera. What cheek! Sameera looked away with a frown and quickly tried to merge with the crowd. The dinner was delicious. As she was enjoying the last scoop of her ice cream, she saw him again a few rows ahead. A shiver ran through her. Bidding a hasty farewell to the bride and bridegroom and the friends who still surrounded them, Sameera retreated.

She looked behind her shoulders to make sure nobody was following. Balancing herself on her stilettos she walked as fast as she could, hoping against hope, to find some means of transport. She was lucky, indeed. An autorikshaw pulled up near her. Sitting in the speeding autorikshaw, she spotted him near one of the junctions once again. When they had to stop near the traffic light, the motorbike man stationed himself almost parallel to the autorikshaw. He was grinning at her and his gestures, oh God, were far from decent! By now, Sameera was almost faint with fear. With a hammering heart, she paid the driver the fare and without waiting for the change, ran into the house. Her mother looked at her with surprise. Her face was death-pale. Sweat tricked down her face, making a mess of her makeup.

'Sameera, what is wrong with you?' her mother cried.

Sameera clung to her mother. 'Ma, somebody has been chasing me. He shadowed me all through the evening. He is there right now. I saw him getting off his motorbike,' Sameera sobbed.

'Chandu, come down at once! Call the neighbours. Is Jaggu Dada in? Shout for him. A rowdy has come to our doorstep, chasing Sameera.'

Father wheeled himself out into the courtyard. Meera came running out. Chandu charged in, armed with his hockey sticks. Jaggu Dada sauntered in, pulling out his deadly knife. 'Where is he, Sameera, just point him out. We will make mince-meat out of him.'

'Chandu bhaiya, there he is. Across the road. He is coming down the pavement.'

'Where? Sameera, where is he?'

'There he is! He has moved to the kiosk. Over there. Don't you see?'

'Where, Sameera? Where?'

The Warp and the Weft

No strength left. Even to toss and turn. The coarse bed-covers, stiffly starched, feel prickly and strain against the wasted cage-like body. Never knew I had such an angular frame. Folds of flesh, which once sat pretty on me, hugging contours and curves, have fallen off like scales. Sleep-starved eyes move restlessly from the mouldy patch on the wall to the high ceiling, to the grimy blades of the mournfully whirling fan. The night nurse, a soft-spoken young person, moving from bed to bed – dove-like – tries to drug me to sleep. One of those morphine-induced trances! Sacrilege, to call them sleep. A jerk, a thud, cold sweat trickles down the neck. Am I falling out of my body? Back again, on vigil, fighting, braving yet another bout of pain. A muffled moan, a sob, a shrill cry--- I hear my fellow sufferers. The ebb and flow, the cadence of their pain. Outside on the corridor, the heavy footsteps of the watchman mark the milestones of my night.

From the window at the far end of the ward, through the gap in the curtain, I have glimpses of an oblong-shaped blob of a sky and the first white streaks of dawn. The sparrows, nesting in the branches of the gulmohar tree beneath my bedroom window, must be up and chirping, teasing my husband to leave his cosy bed. I hear the familiar rhapsody of the morning rituals. The swish of the broom in the courtyard, now scraping against the gravel, now crackling against a heap of dried leaves. The milkman at the doorsteps, warm and cheerful, wishing a hearty *Ram Ram Bibiji*. The initial hiccups and cough of water as it struggles to escape the pipeline. Tina, my thirteen year old Pomeranian sits curled up on the kitchen floor barking at the squirrel scurrying across the windowpane. I wonder does anyone remember to give the squirrel its quota of grains? The pressure cooker hisses on the stove. A whiff of spice, the delectable trail of cardamom and cloves! Shanku's milkshake swirls and whips in the mini blender. Omelette dotted with black and green pepper bubbles on the pan. Can Gopu's wife, the pretty little thing, take all this on her young shoulders?

I look at the photographs precariously balanced on the top of the trolley--- the one and only piece of furniture around me. The bride and the bridegroom. Gopu looks like a prince--- so tall, all smiles. The bride looks glorious too. The five of us. The pink and white blossoms of the madhumalti hold a canopy for us! The auspicious day when the bride walked in under a shower of rice grains and rose petals. How happy we look! Who could have foreseen the shadows round the corner?

Gopu comes with his wife and stands at my feet. The girl cradles a basket laden with fruit - a duck-shaped cane basket— in her arms. The beady brown eyes, the beak, a dark maroon! Don't they look familiar? Oh! The wonderful holiday we had. My husband and I --- in the hills, a couple of years before the birth of Shanku. I picked up the duck-basket in one of the malls. Where was it hiding all these years? I must have tucked it away in the attic. The bride is familiar with the house.

'Gopu, you don't have to look so mournful. I see rainbows and moonbeams in your eyes and hers. Let your happiness reach out to me. Tell your bride to cut an apple or peel an orange for me. Never mind if she has not taken to Tina. Tina is old and epileptic. Her fits can be scary... It is hard. But that is a wise decision. You must put her to sleep. No.. No .. Don't worry. Shankar has not been carrying tales. I agree with your bride Gopu, Shankar mustn't eat so many chocolates. Yes, he must go for jogging.' I bid them go home. They have lots to catch up with.

My husband walks in. He carries a single rose in his hands, a yellow rose, my favourite and his. How thin and tired he looks! Grief has darkened his face. He cannot bear to touch my head. Underneath the silk scarf, my head looks and feels like a stubble field. A well-meaning optimistic chemotherapist has harvested my luxurious long hair. He holds my hand. His hands are clammy with sweat. I can feel his strain. I urge him to go. His life has to flow to the rhythm of tomorrow. The clock ticks for him. The calendar rolls for him. And I .... Can I compress this moment? Or can I stretch it to infinity...

Today is Alfonsa's birthday. Not really. Her birthday falls in June and today is only the seventh of March. But.... who has the heart to utter the truth—that the little girl may not live until June? The doctors, the nurses, the ward boys, even the sweepers have willingly entered into the conspiracy. At six o'clock in the evening, Alfonsa's school friends are coming to the ward to celebrate her birthday. The ayah and the ward boy have been working since morning. Screens have been shifted to one side, curtains have been changed. They have even managed to retrieve a large rectangular table and a few chairs from the reception lounge. The entire ward is getting ready for the occasion.

All those who are not in excruciating pain have offered to lend a hand in the arrangements. After all, Alfonsa is the youngest inmate and the darling of ward number nine, the purgatory of the terminally ill patients. They know, unlike them, Alfonsa is free from burden, the burden of knowledge, the knowledge of the doom. A chirpy, giggly nine year-old, blissfully happy, who wouldn't like to keep her that way? Even the grumpy old Bhagwanti who keeps screaming and cursing from the neighbouring bed, has a soft corner for little Alfonsa.

Of course their heart goes out to Alfonsa's poor mother— Alfonsa is the only patient who has been allowed an attendant—who sits by her daughter's bedside with red-rimmed eyes and a smouldering heart, taking all the woes on herself. Even when Alfonsa has her fits of fever and bouts of pain, her mother knows how to soothe her. Cradling her in her arms, she croons a song, says a prayer, or tells a story, and Alfonsa soon cheers up or mercifully slips into peaceful sleep.

Two ladies, who have beds opposite to Alfonsa's bed, are busy cutting stars and flowers out of pink and blue sheets of paper. Bhagwanti is sitting up on her bed, chopping apples and guavas. She wants to make, her special fruit chaat for Alfonsa. Another lady is piecing together a rag-doll for Alfonsa. Festivities in ward number nine! The pain and the trauma, the countdown. Have they forgotten it all? The nurses look on, a bit amused, a bit relieved.

Alfonsa's mother makes sure she takes all the items out of the car. Gingerly, she lifts up the cake which has been carefully packed in a cardboard box. Alfonsa had wanted a chocolate cake in the shape of a train. Last year, she had asked for an airplane cake and the year before last, she had insisted on a chariot shaped one. Alfonsa always likes to be on the move. Driving in a speeding car, spinning and swirling in a merry-go-round, she would pluck the air into her mouth and laugh.

This morning while whipping butter and sugar into a smooth cream, Alfonsa's mother had helplessly looked at those saline drops—her own miserable tears, much more than a sprinkle--- falling across the swirling stuff. Vigorously, almost with a violence that surprised her, she kept beating at it until the whole thing, sighing with air bubbles, rose up into one huge mass. No... She couldn't afford to sigh and weep. That would be luxury. Alfonsa had to be kept happy till the end. She should never come to know about the verdict. Even when they were alone, she and her husband had never talked about the countdown. Who knows, the echoes of their despair may somehow creep across to the little girl! They must bear the cross silently, for their daughter's sake. She swiftly folded chocolate and flour into the bowl and shoved the tray into the oven.

She had always enjoyed giving gifts to the children who came for her daughter's birthday. She has chosen something special this time too, something they can keep for long if they wished to cherish the memory of Alfonsa. It is a cute figurine carved out of shining creamy sea shells, of a little girl hugging a tiny guitar to herself and looking up at a tree in full bloom. The little girl looks like a solitary angel, lonely and lost like Alfonsa herself. With an effort, she swallows the rising lump in her throat. Both her hands loaded with baskets, she walks towards the ward.

Alfonsa had come to them like a real angel. She was born to them ten years after their marriage, after years of heart-rending prayers. Finally, when she was born prematurely in the eighth month of her pregnancy, what heartburn both she and her husband had gone through! For the first few days, they had watched her with bated breath like a treasure enclosed in the incubator. Their heart fluttered as they looked on, milk falling into her mouth--- her ridiculously tiny mouth--- drop by drop, from the end of a cotton bud. And later at home, trying to keep her warm with hot water bottles night after night, they had taken turns to sit by her cradle. The premature birth, they had succeeded in harbouring, but the premature death, would they be able to harness it? Tears roll down her cheeks. Oh, Jesus! What kind of a trial is this?

Alfonsa hugs Mamma and peers into the basket. She has been waiting anxiously for Mamma. She tries to rattle off the story of the day in a single breath. The silver cross, tied in a black silk thread pathetically hangs round her bird-like neck. She holds it out to her mother. A birthday gift to Alfonsa from Mother Superior who had come to visit her in the morning. Two of her teachers had also come along. A shining black leather-bound copy of the Bible is lying next to her pillow; it is her class teacher's special gift.

'Mamma, I reminded Mother Superior, she has to hold a special exam for me. Don't you remember she had promised me that? I have missed the annual exam.

If I don't sit for an exam how can I be promoted to the next class?'

Alfonsa's mother winces. Alfonsa doesn't know the annual exams are to start two months from now. What could Mother Superior have said? She wouldn't tell lies. Or was she forced to do so for Alfonsa's sake? Alfonsa's mother looks vaguely at the little hands of her daughter ruffling the gold-rimmed pages of the Bible.

'Mamma, why don't you cut my nails? While talking to Mother Superior my nose bled. The nurse said it is because I scratched my nose.' The nurse standing at the foot of the bed nods her head vigorously, a bit too vehemently, as though she wished to confirm it and looks at the mother helplessly. The message doesn't miss her.

'Mother Superior has promised she would hold a special prayer and light a pair of candles in the church as tall as me,' Alfonsa goes on.

Last Sunday in the church, Alfonsa's mother had asked the Father if it would be all right to call a soothsayer to the hospital. One of her neighbours knew a pious old Brahmin who claimed he could touch and heal.

'There is no harm in trying. Though no miracle can

cure your daughter. It may give you some satisfaction.' Father had smiled at her kindly.

The soothsayer had pulled a cotton wick out of his bundle. Dipping it generously in ghee, he lit it carefully and held it at Alfonsa's head for full five minutes. With his free hand, he felt her pulse and muttered a few words. He threw the live wick into the bowl filled with a blood-red liquid –a concoction of turmeric and lime. Alfonsa enjoyed every bit of the show; especially the sizzling sound of the flame as it fell into the bowl. With that the soothsayer had driven away all evil eyes. So, she was told. Alfonsa was relieved and happy. The Mami next door had sent the holy man to hasten her recovery. But her mother knew too well that neither the soothsayer nor the candles of Mother Superior could ever wave leukaemia away.

The little girls walk in, dressed in their best party frocks. There are a few boys too, smartly turned out. Even Alfonsa has discarded her dull hospital gown and is wearing a white billowy frock trimmed with thin lines of filigree lace. Her friends flock around her and sing the merry 'Happy Birthday to You' tune for her. The aunties sit up on their sick beds and watch the scene with brimming eyes. Alfonsa's parents are busy running around the ward, handing over plates, loaded with sweetmeats and savories.

'Alfonsa, why are you celebrating your birthday? It is not yet June.' It is Preeti, Alfonsa's best friend calling out to her from the other end of the ward.

Alfonsa's mother suddenly stops in her tracks. 'Preeti, don't you know Alfonsa is very sick?' It is Manish, the boy next door, 'She may not survive until June, I heard my mother telling my father.'

Before Alfonsa's mother can rush in and still Manish, he has passed the verdict.

The forks and spoons clatter ominously through the silence. The doctors and nurses look away in confusion. The auntie from the opposite bed breaks into a sob. Alfonsa's mother runs to her daughter's bed and folds her to her bosom. Father walks wearily, abjectly, towards the bed. Alfonsa looks at Preeti and Manish, at the doctors and the nurses and smiles disarmingly.

'Mamma, I will recover. Jesus will take care of me. The monk Alphonso will protect me. The soothsayer said I would live a hundred years. Mother Superior said she would light hundred candles -each one as tall as me – and pray for me.' Alfonsa strokes her mother's head and holds her heaving body in her tender arms. Father looks on with unblinking eyes.

'Get away you dogs, I won't leave a pie for you. You want to see the end of me. Who told you I am dying? I won't go for a long time yet. Bhagwanti will give you the surprise of your life. Me dying? Maré méré dushman! Let death come to the whole lot of you, my enemies.' When Bhagwanti kicked her feet and pounded on her chest and screamed, the nurses and the ward boys had a tough time. They had to tie her arms and put her legs into straps and pin her down to the bed. She would spit at them and curse them.

Bhagwanti was not always violent. This happened only on the days when she had a visitor.

Bhagwanti told the social workers who came on their weekly rounds for counselling that she had no one except a son who had settled in the U.K. But once in two weeks or at least once in a month, visitors came for her who called themselves her relatives. Despite Bhagwanti's curses and abuses, there was one young man who patiently called on her every Sunday. Nandu came and stood by her bed with folded hands. Bhagwanti wouldn't let him touch her feet. She would ward him off and scream.

'Badi Ma ? Who is that? I am not your Ma. You are no son of mine. Lalaji wouldn't look at my son. What was wrong with my Kishore? He was a bit dark. As if this pahadi chooha--- this mountain rat is a prince! Pygmy sized, pale like death! You have come to see if I am dead or not? Where is that bitch that gave birth to you? Dead and gone, isn't it? But I am still here. That is it. There is someone above who sees every thing. Brought down from the hills to sweep the floor and wash vessels, that puny bit of a girl would dare to eat from my plate!'

Nandu wouldn't utter a word. He would just dodge the missiles she threw at him, the apples and oranges he had carried for her. He would pick them up one by one and patiently put them back into the plastic bag. With folded hands, he would resume his place at the feet of his Badi Ma.

'You must be a mém, look at your golden hair and blue eyes.' That was Bhagwanti to one of the counsellors. Bhagwanti had a soft corner for Monica, a girl in her early twenties, tall and fair, always dressed in slacks or jeans. She would let the girl oil her hair and plait it.

'My Kishore must have found someone like you for himself. I didn't want to send him abroad. But Kishore was so stubborn; he went on a hunger strike. He wanted to give the agent ten thousand rupees for his passport and visa. Lalaji wouldn't give him the money. But how could I see my child starving? I sold my jewellery and gave the money to Kishore. Lalaji came to know about it only later. He dared not question me. After all, the jewellery was what my father had given me.'

'Does Kishore come to see you? Where is he now?'

'In the last ten years he has not come even once to India. I have heard things about him. He has married a Mem. And he called his blood parents to London.'

'Blood parents? What does that mean?'

'Kishore was not born from my womb. You know I carry within me arid land. When the mango tree which my saas, my mother-in-law made me plant behind the courtyard, didn't bear fruit even after five years, I heard hushed whispers around me. Even the champak that I tended with all my love never bloomed. 'You are a banjh, a barren woman,' the women silently summed me up with their contemptuous eyes. My saas of course used it as a fond name for me. Nothing will grow on her, the accursed one. Even lice would die in her hair. I have heard her telling the neighbours. But something is now growing in me after all. The cancer... isn't it?' Bhagwanti chuckled. Such bitter pronouncements! She wouldn't spare even her own self. How could she be so brutal to herself? A shudder went through Monica.

'Then Kishore is your adopted son?'

'Yes, I adopted him against the wishes of Lalaji. If I had been a little soft, he would have brought home his darling Nandu, born to that slut. My money, my father's money, was a big boon to me. Lalaji couldn't take me lightly. A delicately built, mild-mannered man, he wouldn't have married a sturdy, swarthy woman like me but for my inheritance. I knew that, and made the best use of it. Lalaji sat in baithaks playing cards with young men from the neighbourhood and visited Putli, Nandu's mother, under the cover of night. I knew everything. I couldn't care less. But I kept the keys of the tijori to myself. See it is with me even today.'She pulled out a leather satchel from under her pillow, and shook it in front of Monica. The keys clanked a triumphant chime. She opened the bag and brought out a scroll that looked like a parchment and carefully spread it on the bed.

'This is my will. Do you know why that dog comes sniffing around my bed? '

'But Masi, what will you do with your property?

Can you carry it with you? If Nandu gets it or some other relative gets it, what does it matter?' Monica had entered a forbidden territory.

'Why should I give my precious things to that Vaman? Don't be taken in by his humble looks. He would gladly step on my head and push me down to pataal. I will never ever forgive him. But for him, Lalaji would have loved Kishore. If he had loved Kishore, he wouldn't have gone away. I pleaded with Lalaji to accept him as his son. But he called him an idiot. He sent his Nandu to college and my Kishore, he said, should train himself as a carpenter. A brand new cycle for Nandu to go to college and no money for Kishore to travel to UK to take up the job of a carpenter! So I gave him all my money, all my jewellery. He got his passport, got his visa, bought his ticket and flew away.'

'And what happened to his blood-parents?'

'He is my brother's son. So my brother and Bhabhi are his blood parents, aren't they? They gave me their baby. They gave life to a barren woman. But what a heavy price I was called to pay! Now Kishore takes care of them, his blood parents. And the foster mother has become a thing of the past he would rather not own.'

'Then why don't you make peace with Nandu?'

'Never... I am a mother. It is Kishore who called me mother first and last. I would forgive him anything. My house, my furniture, all the treasures I had hoarded over the years, everything is for him. He will come back. I am waiting for him.'

'What about all those relatives who come to visit you?'

'They are all my Bhabhi's relatives. They want to fleece me. Don't I know them? The apples and guavas they bring for me, I won't touch them. Even a worm trapped in them would coil around my neck.'

'Masi, you know how seriously ill you are. Don't hate people. It will only make you sicker. Why don't you try to forgive?' Monica was trying to do full justice to the job of a counsellor.

'Forgive those wolves? Never.... They wish me only evil. They are waiting for me to die, to scavenge on my wealth.' Bhagwanti clung to her keys and her bag and screamed. 'Maré méré dushman, let my enemies die. Bhagwanti is not going to die. I will give them the surprise of their life...'

Saffron Shades

The porter walked ahead. Briskly. In spite of the load, he was carrying. He was by no means young. Which young man would opt to wear himself out, carrying other people's burden? Especially, these days. In his prime, he must have been a muscular man. But now his shoulders stooped. Telltale varicose veins strained against the blotchy skin of his legs and forearms. My suitcase sat smugly on his turbaned head, and on it was perched the bedroll, strapped and buckled, doubly secured by lengths of ugly looking ropes. With his left hand, he firmly held the precariously balanced bedroll down to the suitcase. On his shoulder, he had slung the bag, bursting with all those goodies mother had so affectionately packed in. Another bag, equally swollen, rested on the crook of his arm and in his free hand he held the huge water can. A house was on move ---on human wheels!

Shouting and pushing, he propelled his way through the milling crowd. So many people! The entire population of the small town seemed to have been let loose on this lousy station. My father walked behind the porter, desperately trying to stretch his steps to match the maze-like movement, the unpredictable detours of the porter. Dodging another head-load of luggage, or ducking under awnings, he had disappeared from our view not once but thrice. Father followed him with watchful eyes, lest he lost sight of his daughter's precious belongings. Mother walked behind father, with her eyes as usual glued to her husband's feet. She held the baby —wrapped in flannels in a cone-shaped bundle— to her bosom, protecting him from the jostling crowd. I walked behind mother with Bindu trotting by my side, her tiny fingers locked in mine in a firm grip.

As the cartoon-like procession approached the ladies' compartment, our leader slackened his pace. Blocking the narrow entrance to the compartment, stood a middle-aged lady, fat and broad-shouldered. She was desperately trying to heave herself up on to the high pedestal-like steps and our porter impatiently, almost rudely, called out to her. 'Out of the way. It is not your bungalow...' Two young girls who stood giggling at the doorway came to her rescue. The moment they pulled her up, the porter hoisted my suitcase and the bedroll on the steps and dived in. The luggage, deposited safely on the berth, the porter took leave of us. He gave me a big salaam. Obviously, father had given him a generous tip.

Father hurriedly spread the bedroll on the lower berth. We simply had to take possession of the berth.

With the baby in my arms and Bindu at my side, I couldn't have spent half a day and one full night squatting on my seat. If only I had managed to reserve my seats! I need not have stepped into this lousy ladies' compartment. But the SOS had come from my husband only the other day. At such short notice, even through a minister's quota, I couldn't have dreamt of wangling a seat for myself. I couldn't blame my husband though. He didn't know until the last moment that Bindu had to submit herself for an interview. After having donated a mighty sum towards the building fund and having tried all sources of influence to cultivate the school authorities, he had not anticipated such a calamity. But our five-year-old daughter's future was hanging by a thread. Well, if she had a chance to get into the best convent of the city, she shouldn't miss it. The day after tomorrow, come what may, Bindu had to be there. So here I was, huddled in a corner, travelling like a tramp in the ladies' compartment.

It was time for the train to move. Mother's eyes had already welled up. As though her grandchildren and daughter were going to another continent, crossing oceans and mountains! She reluctantly put the baby down on my lap. Silly! My eyes grew moist too. Even I hated farewells as much as mother did. 'Don't let

Bindu run around. Keep an eye on the bags kept under the seats. Don't buy any food from outside,' father repeated his instructions for the third time. He still took his daughter to be a kid. Mother looked at the woman who sat on the opposite seat with obvious disapproval.

'Look at the shimmering outfit. What a garish red! What does she think she is carrying on her head? A mini garden? Doesn't look a decent sort. Be careful.' Mother whispered. The station-gong chimed, announcing the departure of the train. Mother and father hurriedly got out of the compartment. As the train whistled out of the platform, I looked around. Mother was right. The red apparition across the seat did look a suspicious character. The girls, who sat in twos and threes on the upper berths and to the left and right of the woman, looked strange too. I noticed they had dholaks with them. Seemed to be dancing girls. Or a singing troupe? The woman must be the manager. Or the madam? I wondered. Bindu's admiring eyes were taking in the colour and glitter of the scene – the tinsel dupattas, the bangles, the anklets, and the shimmering bright bindi. The girls, I noticed were trying to attract her attention through body language. I held Bindu firmly to my side, signalling to her with my eyes not to respond to their overtures.

The train puffed and howled past small and big stations. Darkness had already descended. Often at a distance, I could see a cluster of flickering lights --- perhaps a hamlet or a settlement--- like fireflies flitting past in the dark. Bindu, after struggling for an hour with a pair of sandwiches, had at last curled herself to sleep at my feet. The baby took his feed, moved his eyes vaguely around and smiled. He shook his pink-tipped fingers, folded tightly into fists, kicked his tiny legs for a while and then yawned and quietly went back to sleep.

Madam was in full command of her forces. Trunks and bedrolls and attaches were dragged around the aisle between the two berths and soon a mini dining hall materialised in the compartment. Through half-closed eyes, I watched the girls fondly waiting on their auntie. Delectable food peeped out of lotus leaf packs! The flavour of food – pungent pickles, sweets and savouries fried in desi ghee wafted around the compartment tickling my taste buds. A bit ruefully, I considered, had I responded to their initial attempts to be pally with Bindu, sure, they would have invited me to join their feast. But I was not going to thaw. I turned my back to them and tried to sleep. The girls were in a carnival mood. All night they were awake, chatting, giggling, or singing --- often film songs, occasionally a bhajan or two. One of the girls had a sweet husky voice. Listening to the soft strains of a love song of Radha pining for Krishna on the banks of Jamuna, I dozed off.

With a jerk, I came out of my fitful sleep. The train was no longer rocking us. A lurch, a drag, the wheels screeched to a halt. My hands reached out for baby and Bindu. They were safe and sleeping peacefully . It was still dark outside, wee hours of morning. We had not stopped at a station. It could be that the signals were down. Or we could be waiting for another train to cross us and clear the line? Suddenly, there was a big commotion in the compartment. The girls were shouting at someone, probably an intruder.

'Who are you? Where have you come from? This is not even a station...' They were protesting.

'I am coming from the next bogie. It is a general compartment and so crowded... I was pushed out... They told me to try my luck in the ladies' compartment...' A whining voice was pleading with them. Through sleepy eyes, I watched the scene. The intruder stood at the feet of Madam who was fast asleep – sprawled on the floor covering herself with a flowery bedsheet– an old woman, clad in a saffron coloured sari. In her hands, she held a shabby cloth bag.

'Let me sit here....' she said pointing at the harmonium which looked like a box, deceptively covered with a rectangular piece of cloth.

The girls now fell up on her like a pack of wolves. 'No... No.. Get away. There is no room here....' They screamed at her.

'Just a little space to squeeze in please...' She looked at them beseechingly. A gesture of defiance (against whom?) or a spontaneous response to her pleas, I didn't know what it was that prompted me. But to my own surprise – as though I had something to prove – I found myself rising to the occasion. Shifting Bindu a little more to my side, I bade the frightened lamb to sit down on my seat.

'Don't do that. She had crept in from the dark. You never know these saffron creatures,' The girls now turned to me.

My green signal obviously renewed her sagging energy. With one hop, she crossed Madam's feet, came over to my corner and settled down near Bindu. It was now for the girls to turn their back to me. The old lady placed a gentle hand on my sleeping children as though blessing them. Then she sat facing the aisle like a statue with eyes closed in deep meditation. In the morning, I offered her some coffee. But she vigorously shook her head and declined. Later, I saw her accepting the banana which Bindu held out to her. They seemed to be warming towards each other. I was glad Bindu was occupied. It kept her out of mischief.

The old lady had taken out her beads. Her lips moved silently, mouthing a mantra or a prayer and her fingers in a synchronising movement went over and over the beads. Bindu was watching her with rapt attention, obviously fascinated. What was she doing with her beads? Bindu was asking her chirpily. She was counting the name of Rama a thousand times, that was what she told the child. What was thousand? Bindu turned to me. Oh! The best way to refresh her mind with the intricacies of numbers. After all, she had to face the fateful interview. Ten times you count hundred, it is very simple, I told her, you arrive at thousand. That reminded her of her abacus. She insisted on taking it out of the bag. So the pair sat together, one pushing and probing her smooth beads, pink and green and white and the other going over the tiny frizzes of her black beads.

Bindu, kept busy, I turned to the baby and changed his nappies, I mopped and powdered him. A few more hours. We would be in Bombay. The corridors were now less crowded. Cooped up in my seat I felt stiff all over. With the baby in my arms I strolled up and down the corridor. The train was slowing down. Signals were down once again, I thought. Suddenly I heard a shrill cry. I knew it was Bindu. Panic-stricken, I ran back. Bindu was sitting with the black beads in her hand and was screaming. 'She gave me the black beads and took my gold chain off,' Bindu said between sobs.

We could see the hastily retreating form of the saffron woman near the doorway. One of the girls ran after her. By then the train was already on the move. The girl walked through the connecting bogies and brought the guard and a policeman all the way back. The guard said they had been on the lookout for the saffron lady, for days. She had got away for the third time this month.

'Don't worry, sister, we will recover your chain.' With my head bowed, I sank into my corner. I couldn't face the *we warned you* look written large on the face of the girls. What a fool I had been. She could have even snatched my babies.

Through the window, I absently looked at the arid

landscape we were passing through. Lampposts and billboards were emerging into view. We were approaching a big town. Might be the last major halt before the final destination. The girls were putting their things together. They dragged their trunks and carefully carried the musical instruments to the door. As Madam and her girls filed out of the compartment, they smiled and waved to Bindu and me. Shame-faced I responded to them mechanically. Bindu crossed over to the empty opposite seat and put her head out of the window and waved them good bye. Trolleys carrying newspapers and magazines, food stuff and fancy items wheeled past our window. A vendor came trotting, calling out his wares.

'Halwa lo... Halwa.... Kesar Halwa...' It was a young boy with spindly limbs. He was just a child. Couldn't have been more than ten. On his shoulders, he was carrying a glass case lined with square pieces of halwa, translucent, of a glossy saffron shade, each piece topped with a tiny nut. It was colourful and appealing to the eye. Bindu suddenly put her hand out and beckoned him.

'No.. No.... These sweets are not good for you...'I frowned at her. I knew she was in a peevish mood. But I wasn't prepared for such a showdown.

'I want to have it... I want to have it.' She stamped her foot and kicked the bags around.

The boy lingered on, obviously, encouraged and hopeful. But I wasn't going to give in. 'What has grandpa told you? No food from outside... He has warned you. These sweets are not clean. They will upset your stomach. You cannot afford to fall ill....' I had to be very firm with her.

'No... Memsaheb– my sweets are very clean. They are home-made. My mother herself has prepared them. They are the best in the town... He claimed proudly. Please buy a few pieces. Since morning I had not sold a single one....' He pleaded.

I pulled Bindu away from the window. By now she was howling. Pretending to be very busy with the baby, I turned my back to the vendor. As the train was slowly drawing its length, getting ready to move out of the station, I saw Bindu once again at the window. The skinny hands of the boy were reaching out to Bindu. I was horrified. He had slipped into her hand a piece of halwa wrapped neatly in a plastic sheet. My heart hammered. He called out to me from outside.

' Mem saab.... Don't throw the sweet away. Baby won't fall ill...' He must have seen me struggling with the clasps of my purse. 'No... No.... Memsaab I don't want money.... Let sister have the sweet...'

He was now running with the train. I was dazed. I put my hand out of the window. I wanted to touch his gentle hand. But the train had already picked up speed. I stuck my head out of the window and through a film of tears, watched the receding silhouette of the boy until it turned to a tiny speck and disappeared from my view.

You and I

What are you thinking about Rita? Are you sad? Are you worried or are you just lost in thoughts? You stand under the flickering, fluorescent lamp, on the terrace of your double-storeyed house, like an angel without wings. The powder blue night-gown outlines your firm and soft symmetry conspicuously, like that of a mannequin. Are you thinking about your husband who has gone away to Singapore. Or, are you thinking about the fourth stillborn child you had delivered in the fifth year of your marriage? Just think of it, if your husband had not ventured his way to promising new lands looking for wealth, you wouldn't have been standing on the spacious terrace of this palatial house.

When you skip on the dew-washed grass in your garden, when you go chasing the dragon files out of your rose beds, I know your husband isn't there to hold your hands. Nor is he there to share the four-course lunch, so fastidiously prepared by the army of attendants fawning around you. You tend your garden, you scold your servants, you flip through the shabby leaves of the paperback novels dropped at home by the library on wheels. You fret and fume, sigh and moan away your mornings and evenings. I know all this. But what about those long blue envelopes the postman brings you every week? Your husband's loving arms must be reaching out to you through them. Doesn't he croon all those sweet nothings you long to hear? Or, has he stopped sending you letters? You are surprised. How do I know so much about you?

Sitting by the casement, the pigeon hole window, at the south wing of my wife's tharavade, the family house, I have been watching you stealthily, day after day. At dawn, when sparrows flap their wings on the wooden shutters and rouse me from my sleepless nights. At night, when the wind drums against the rusted iron bars and laughing at my lot, flies back into the night. My wife has never come to know about my antics. Or else, she would have closed the shutters forever. She might have even pulled down the window and plastered the wall.

I know, Rita, you couldn't have seen me. For, like a thief, I sat in the dark, hiding myself in my own house– no, in the tharavade of my wife– with unkempt beard and unruly hair. But I kept looking at you, day after day, night after night, and my wife knew nothing about it. My wife, Rama's and Uma's mother, is pious and godfearing. She lights the lamp every evening on the tulasi shrine and sits on the veranda with her daughters, and together, they chant shlokas — the Vishnu stuti and the Siva stuti. The stereo music, which comes bellowing from your double-storeyed house, I know, infuriates her. What does she know about lilting rock or classy jazz?

Heathen, crazy, indecent, she brainwashes her impressionable daughters. The ewe lambs will bolt out of the ropes very soon. I am waiting for the day. Rama, the eldest would be the first to do so. The other day, I saw her huddled in a corner, lost in Dostoevsky. She broods over crime and punishment. The moisture I see in her eyes whenever she looks at me, (Oh! my dear daughter!) falls on me like a balm, more soothing than the cool mixture of herbs and clay which she used to massage on to my scalp, so kindly, those early days of my depression. She could come to me then. I was only a depressed man, not yet branded. Rama is like me or I am like Rama. Like her, I love books. She loves books like me.

But now, I read only these huge ledgers and files. I count, add, subtract, divide and multiply and check the entries. I cannot afford to make another mistake. My father thought I was crazy to think I could make my living by writing. Whenever I sat on the highest branch of the mango tree, greedily reading my books, my brothers used to throw stones at me. They said they were trying to get at the green mangoes and mother never punished them.

When I failed to get entry into an engineering college, my father decided I should enter a bank. Even that was not very easy. He knew some powerful guys. So I found myself behind a cash counter, counting and doling out crisp and crumpled, used and abused, stained and sullied currency notes.

How did that big discrepancy come about? I am sure it was not my mistake. I worked very hard and I was very careful those days. My job had brought me respect and recognition. In my house I was a *someone* now. My father was happy, I bought blankets and his favourite brand of cigarettes for him. My wife gave me dewy looks whenever I brought a new sari for her. My children came running to the door and clung to me every first day of the month when I carried in a bag full of toys for them. The power and the glory of money; I relished every bit of it. I was pleased with my own self. And I wished things to stay that way. So I was punctual at work, extra cautious and hard working. I had a clear bright vision of my future. I had to build a house for my wife; I had to get my daughters married.

How could I have been careless when I was gearing myself for promotions? I am sure, I had not made any miscalculations. I know it was my best friend who had done the mischief. I remember very well, he had relieved me at the counter for twenty minutes that day. Those twenty minutes had mauled me for life. Of course, he denied it when questioned in the court. I was a small man. I carried my innocence mutely like a cross. My father paid a huge sum to save me. He couldn't survive the shock. So many fingers pointing at me! My brothers and sisters shunned me. My wife glared at me accusingly. I crept to my corner, in the south wing of my wife's tharavade and read and reread, checked and rechecked the huge ledgers.

'Those silly notebooks! He tells me they are the bank records,' I heard my wife telling her darling brother and they laughed.

But these are really the bank ledgers. How can I convince them? They think I have gone mad. When I snap at the flies and sweep the spider and cockroach away from my corner, even the maids laugh at me. Uma, my younger daughter, looks at me in fear. I haven't harmed any one of them; I will not harm any one of them. Still, they keep away from me. I am a branded man. I am a man who has lost his job; I am a man who has lost his mind. Only Rama perhaps understands how I feel. Rama is like me, or I am like Rama. A victim, an outsider, I sit here in this corner, in the south wing of my wife's tharavade, silently counting, minutes, hours, months and years. And I stealthily look at you, Rita, through this pigeon hole-window. My wife knows nothing about it. Or else, she would pull down the window and plaster the wall.

My wife is smart, efficient; she runs the house like a queen. She counts coconuts, separates a few, dries them in the sun, sends them to the mill for fresh oil. She measures the paddy, stores the rice and rules the servants with an iron hand. Friends and relatives are all praise for her and they click their tongues, and condole the life in death of her criminal, ineffectual husband. They marvel at her patience and generosity. She will be blessed even in her next janma, for carrying this burden —me. How many women would have tolerated such a man, with an unruly beard and unkempt hair, snapping at flies, peering through ledgers, even though he sits silently in a dark corner, in the unused wing of this sprawling house?

Rita, let me ask you again, what are you thinking about? Those long blue envelopes, are they not regular any longer? Or instead of bringing you comfort, do they now bring nightmares to you? You fear, your husband had moved far away from you? You are alarmed; he has found another woman who would give him his heir apparent? Your heart bleeds when you think of the four stillborn babes you had borne for him. You wish to plead with him to give you a chance a fifth time. But you know, you wish in vain. It is a hopeless situation.

I have seen you playing with your neighbour's children. From the hutment across the road, you bring the half-naked, starving children, bathe them and dress them in new clothes. You make them sit on your lap and feed them. How many times have I watched you hugging them, holding them to your heart? You have a mother's heart. What if the babes from your womb have not survived? Open your heart, a mother's heart, to the children of the world. Be kind to them, be kind to me. Hold me in your arms as you hold those babes and wipe my tears. Be kind to a man who sits curled in a corner like a bundle of soiled clothes.

The man who stands behind the bars of this casement, with unruly hair and unshaven beard – is he a mad man? You, who stand on the terrace of your double-storeyed house, grieving for your stillborn babes, are you an accursed soul? Your mansion where, in the absence of your husband, men, young, middle-aged and old, come and go at all odd hours. Is it an entertainment house? My wife, Rama's and Uma's mother, says so and thinks so. Her contempt for you only makes me more concerned for you. Jesus shielded Mary Magdalene from those who stoned her. Who would save you from my wife and all those who think like my wife?

Rita, don't be sad. You mean a lot to me. You are my mother, you are my sister, you are my sweetheart, and you are all that, and much more to me. You comfort me; I will comfort you. I will keep the pigeonhole window of the south wing of my wife's tharavade open for you. Will you come unobtrusively, in the night, without letting my wife know? Let us go together into the night; let us get lost in darkness. How about it? Will you come?

Stories hum within my head. I see stories spinning all around me. Which is your story? Which is mine? Is their story different from ours?

Retreat

What started as a drizzle, had now turned into a sharp shower. Soon, it would be pouring. Bright sunny mornings. Cloudy afternoons. As evenings descended, lightning flashed, thunder rumbled and heavy rain was ushered in. This had been the routine for the last fortnight or so. Well, you couldn't expect dry days during a season of monsoon. The car moved sluggishly on the wet road. The peak - hour traffic carrying homeward, people, who were work-weary or work-crazy, were as usual, moving at a snail's pace. The rain had further slowed down the movement. The wipers swished back and forth across the windshield with a rhythm of their own.

The four lanes of the road, to the left and to the right, to the back and to the front, were choked with a cavalcade of cars. He had been moving on first gear for the last half an hour. A bumper to bumper crawl. After the next traffic light where the road forked, there would be some relief. Back home, father wouldn't have approved the way he was using the gears. When he taught him how to drive – most reluctantly of course, for he never could trust his young son with his proud possession – he had told him to use the lower gears as sparingly as he could. Obviously, to save on fuel. But Manohar did not need to worry on that score. The multinational computer firm for which he worked, was committed to reimburse his fuel expenses.

By the time the car turned the bend and moved towards Federal Hills, the rain had subsided. Except for the watchman, the apartment block was almost deserted. He parked the car in the basement, picked up the briefcase and the shopping bags and raced up the stairs two at a time. Sami had told him how important it was, especially for a busy executive like him, to exercise his limbs. Avoid using elevators, he had advised him. As he was turning the key on his door he saw the Chinaman coming out of the opposite flat, his petite wife and doll-like daughter in tow. All three of them waved at him, in what looked like a synchronised, computerised gesture. Fortunately or unfortunately, his neighbourly relations with them did not stray beyond such formal greetings.

As soon as he entered the apartment, he threw the briefcase down on the sofa, emptied the shopping bags and lined the contents one by one on the table – cartons and cans, bottles and trays of frozen food. His granny would have fainted had she seen him eating out of these tins and cans, and of course, with renewed vigour, would have taken afresh the campaign for a bride for her dear grandson. Manohar chuckled to himself.

The tie, which had been choking him all day, was pulled out and flung on the bed. The answering machine on the bedside table was blinking furiously at him with a formidable number nine flashing on its laminated display. Nine people had tried to besiege his privacy on the eve of a long weekend. Or, as Sami says, he should take to positive thinking and look at the brighter side. Nine friends had taken pains to plan his weekend for him! As he had anticipated or feared, eight calls were from well-wishing friends who wanted him to join them for a picnic or a lunch or a dinner. Most of these well-wishers, when they extended such gracious invitations to him, had a sister or a daughter or a niece in mind, he ruefully reminded himself. Obviously, they had not yet reached that higher stage in life, where they could see things without a motive. As perhaps a person like Sami had. Once again, as Sami says, why be critical of people? The ninth call was from Sami himself. He wished to remind him of the retreat scheduled to commence on Saturday at Macmillan Highlands.

Back home, he had never cared much for retreats. Frankly speaking, before he had come to this dream country, he had no idea what a retreat was like. Of course, he was literate enough to know the dictionary meaning of the word. But he had never suspected it could hold the key to a magic world. People around him, sure enough, seem to think so. Weekdays just flew in a swirl of meetings and marketing rounds. It was incredible, how people found so much energy— to move heaven and earth— to organise such paradisal weekends.

Even in the corporate world, *retreat* had now become and established itself as a buzzword. A few months ago, Manohar's company held a retreat in a farmhouse in the suburbs. Oh! You should have seen how directors, presidents, and managers came in Bermudas and Nike, played Frisbee and cricket on the sprawling lawns, and had informal chats with the staff over a potluck lunch. Manohar remembered that when he had just joined the company, the President had given him a pep talk: play cleverly on the human aspect of the human resources pledged under you. He had intriguingly revealed to him some of the secrets of the trade. But the retreat organised by Sami was not a motivating gimmick. He had promised a spiritual experience - beautiful pathways to harmony and peace.

Sami was the president of the local Gita Mandalam. Manohar thought highly of him not simply because he had all the trappings of the Guru – a well-built physique, a flowing silver-streaked beard, a metallic voice, small but bright and compelling eyes, and a fund of knowledge. In the premises of the Lakshmi Narayan temple, he had listened to Sami's discourses. And they had been real eye-openers for him. What he had to say about meditation and mantra enthralled him. Back home, he had not thought about inner journeys. His Sanskrit teacher had never bothered to tell him that mantra meant the protection of the mind. Granny had told him to repeat, parrot-like, *Om Namah Shivaya.* Sitting on the marble floor, on a square piece of red carpet, when Sami demonstrated the vibrations of the syllables on the tongue, on the throat, on the heart and its final descent to Paravani, to the innermost depths of one's Being, Manohar felt elated. Sami's eloquence transformed all those platitudes and clichés - which, back home, he had guffawed at – into living experiences. Detachment, karma and kundalini assumed new meanings.

Saturday morning, promptly at ten, he arrived at the retreat. Sami personally came out to receive him. Young girls stood at the entrance in colourful ethnic costumes. They sprinkled rose water on him and dotted his forehead with sandalwood paste. Sami told him, two genuine godmen had arrived to give discourses from homeland. One of the most renowned danseuses of India, a Bharata Natyam exponent, had come all the way from Madras. He pointed to a corner where, surrounded by some people under a tree, sat an astrologer. Jasmine flowers had been specially flown in from the Tirupati Hills, incense sticks from Pondicherry and alphonsoes from Bombay had just arrived, he informed Manohar with great enthusiasm. The array of food on the decorated tables was authentic too. As he was thanking Sami for a very satisfying spiritual experience, Sami extended a very special invitation to him for the next weekend. Sami wished Manohar to share a meal with him at his place. Not a bad idea. He would like to see his Guru in his natural surroundings. Moreover, it was an honour to be a guest at his home.

Sami lived about forty kilometres away from the city centre. It was a Sunday. Traffic moved smoothly and he enjoyed his long ride. He took the new express highway that had been recently thrown open. Moving on a perfect road, flanked by the rugged walls of the ridge, it was a lovely ride. By noon, he reached Sami's cottage. As expected Sami's cottage was sparsely but neatly furnished. Beautiful reed mats were spread on the hall. The walls were covered with framed portraits of gods and goddesses. There were paintings of Vivekananda and Tagore in his study room. He said his daughter had painted them.

Manohar enjoyed the excellent vegetarian lunch that was served to him with traditional hospitality. Sami's wife stood around the table affectionately coaxing him to have a little more chutney, a few more stuffed brinjals. Once or twice, she dropped her voice and said confidentially, all these tasty dishes had been prepared by her daughter. The daughter stood at the doorway near the kitchen, rather bored and disinterested, carrying the dishes in and out of the kitchen whenever her mother summoned her. She was not very young. Had a pinched, worrying sort of a face, as though nothing had ever gone right with her.

After lunch, Sami and Manohar relaxed on the floor mat. Sami pulled out family albums to show him photos of his father and grandfather. While dusting the covers of the albums, he casually asked him how he had liked the concert given by his daughter at the retreat. It was her debut performance. She had learnt Carnatic music from real masters, he added. Oh, Sami too...so, Sami too had his motives and attachments. Manohar laughed inwardly but he tried to sound enthusiastic and turned the pages of the album attentively. Sami's grandfather looked hefty and rather crude. He wore a turban on his head and on his forehead there was a huge tilak. With his hands tightly folded across his chest he was sitting at the edge of a chair as though any moment he was ready to take to his heels. Though he had carefully tucked his feet under his dhoti, a pair of his naked toes had not escaped the camera. Sami had told Manohar, his grandfather had come to Malaya to work as an overseer in a rubber estate. Manohar guessed what the actual credentials of the man must have been. He must have come from India to work in the estates as a humble labourer.

There was another old photograph, slightly discoloured at the corners. That was Sami's father. His hair was neatly cropped. He wore no turban, and he wore a light coloured tie and a black coat over his white dhoti. He proudly displayed his feet for they were neatly clad in well-polished leather shoes. Sami's father, Manohar knew, had been the personal assistant of an Englishman who had been the manager of one of the rubber estates. He was leaning on the carved head of a walking stick as though he were emulating one of his master's tricks. Sami himself had risen much higher than his forefathers and father. He had a British degree and had held a prestigious position in the federal government.

As he was looking curiously at the blonde on the next page, Sami intervened.

'Oh! That is Sandra. She is German. My son and she are living together He went to England for his engineering degree. He now lives in London. He refuses to leave the British Isles to come home. I don't know whether he will marry the girl or not. She is in fact his third girl friend. You know what these youngsters are. I have learnt my lessons. Let them be what they are. It is always better to be gracious. Don't you think so?'

Yes indeed! How liberal...no...how detached Sami was! Manohar gave him one of his charming smiles and nodded, once again diplomatically.

The next weekend – Manohar was fifty kilometres away from the city in the resort of one of his close friends. It was an exclusive club open only to the cream of the elite. Manohar was sitting idly with his friend in a deserted corner in the bar. All of a sudden, for no reason at all, he sprang up from his stool. A middle-aged man who sat meditating over his goblet, as importantly as Socrates pondering over his hemlock, opened his eyes wide and looked around. Manohar clasped the tall crystal glass with both hands and ceremoniously held it high up in the air. He shouted at the top of his voice. Three cheers to Sami...

Fulfilment

The train would stop only for a minute at the station. He slung the video camera on his shoulders and with his right foot, pushed the heavy suitcase towards the door. The co-passengers looked at him curiously. The airline baggage tags on the suitcase and the camera were enough to brand him, no to identify him, as an N.R.I who was on a brief visit to India. Panikkar master was sure to be there. Standing at the doorway, he scanned the shabby length of the platform. As a little boy, he had stood here to welcome the first train that had come puffing in, preening like a peacock to this town.

Teacher, Gopi is given two flags and I have only one.

Foolish kid, you want to wave flags with both the hands like a machine?

Gopi, come, we will stand in the front. I want to be near the engine.

You won't be allowed to be in the front. You know you are the tallest boy.

Okay, we will stand here and when the minister steps down the compartment we will cheer him.

Look... look... there... the train is coming. But where is the engine? And no lights!

Dumb wit, why should there be a light during the day?

I mean I can't see its eye.

Children, the engine is decked up like a beautiful bride. Bashfully, with her brilliant eyes veiled by the garlands, she swings into the station.

What is Malayalam teacher saying? Is he reciting a poem?

If the engine is a bride, where is the bridegroom?

Devayani, can you talk of nothing but a bride and a bridegroom?

Stand on attention. As soon as the train comes to a stop, start throwing the flowers.

That is the no-nonsense drillmaster. Is that the minister? It is a lady. She is so fair!

Children, she is Chacha Nehru's daughter. Indira Gandhi. She is one of the most beautiful women of the world.

If our history teacher thinks so it must be true. She knows a lot.

Let us wave our flags with all our might to please the most beautiful lady of the world.

Gopi, Swami cannot even stand properly; his hands are

always shaking. Do you think he can break the coconut in one stroke?

I don't know why they made him the mayor. Such an old man!

Devayani, stop giggling. Swami will only touch the coconut symbolically.

Our headmaster will break it. Now keep quiet.

What does music teacher mean by symbolic?

Stop muttering. Look, the coconut has burst into two equal halves.

Let us shower flowers.

Silence!

The minister speaks.

Why is she talking – shishi - in English?

The man standing next to her will translate her speech for you. Don't worry. That is the English teacher.

Ugh! Devayani, simply because you are three years older than us don't bully us. Stop poking me with the flower plate.

Gopi turned his head sharply to protest. That was when the belt had snapped and the over-sized shorts that he had borrowed from me had threatened to slip down. Precisely at that moment, the minister said Jai Hind and seemed to look straight at Gopi and I. We saw her beautiful face, a flaming red. She was screaming at the top of her voice. We didn't know, for what! Had she seen Gopi struggling with his belt?

The man standing beside her rushed forward and thundered, 'Madam is annoyed because you didn't call out Jai Hind.' But we didn't know she wanted us to say Jai Hind!

"Come on, children, sisters and brothers, say three times, Jai Hind"

Jai Hind!

'Suren! I am so moved, you have not forgotten our old way of greeting! You seem to have really missed India. Haven't you? Jai Hind!'

Suren looked straight into Panikkar master's eyes. The same khadi jubba with the flap on the right shoulder in the fashion of the late fifties. As usual, he had a towel thrown around his neck like a scarf and held the snuffbox tightly enclosed in the fist of his right hand. But for his bald head, he looked almost the same. Was he still the Good Samaritan of the town? Yes, of course. The very fact that Mash--- how easily the familiar way in which they used to address the teacher had come back to him— had taken pains to arrange a fair sale of their last bit of property, was proof enough.

'Look around carefully Suren. Our sleepy little town is not what you had left years ago. There are factories and hospitals. We even have a medical college here where students from north, east and west come, paying huge amounts of donation. Education has now become a business. Forget all the high and mighty things I used to tell you people. Money, money... that is all what matters.'

Suren was marking the changes all right. From the huge billboards, or hoardings as he used to call them earlier, near the station, seductive females smiled at him, sporting all kinds of things, from Nescafe and medicines to undergarments! There was even a life-size poster of Michael Jackson posing in front of a goggle shop. 'Gifts for your loved ones on Valentine's day,'- said another hoarding. 'Step into Sweetheart.' Valentine's day... Suren didn't realise, he had been reading aloud but Mash had heard him.

'Yes, for the college students every day is a Valentine's day. You should come here in the evenings, you will see pairs and pairs strolling around the railway line.' Suren acknowledged Mash's explanation with an absentminded nod. Valentine's day.... It rang a bell in his mind. The ping-pong table and the reading room in the court club.... It was Gopi who had discovered *Far from the Madding Crowd,* playing hide and seek among a heap of Malayalam novels which were carelessly dumped in a corner. To read Hardy added to one's status. So they read the novel patiently, from cover to cover, though it took them almost a month. That was the first time they had heard about Valentine's day.

'Suren, we should send a Valentine to Devayani.' Gopi came out with one of his brilliant ideas. Everyone knew Devayani was very conscious of her looks. She had a pockmarked face and when she reached her teens, pimples invaded her lack-lustre cheeks with a mad fury. When she tried to squeeze out and erase the pimples, she developed, unfortunately, tiny warts all over her face. Suren had always thought, she had soft affectionate eyes and a gentle smile. But she felt awful about herself and knew with these looks, she had no chance whatsoever in the matrimonial market.

'What rubbish! Devayani would never know what a Valentine is.'

'That is where Suren, you need brains, which I have, and you don't. We will make a *localised* Valentine card"

They did make one and sent it across, but with no signature. Yet, there were enough hints to suggest who her admirer was. Holding their sides, they watched her going to the temple exactly at six in the evening, for one full week at a stretch, with a red hibiscus pinned in her hair- as was enjoined by the card— to meet the drillmaster. Gopi and Suren had their share of laughter and they also had a few nervous moments. They knew Devayani was quite capable of confronting the drillmaster and asking him for an explanation. When the drillmaster went away, quite unexpectedly on transfer, Gopi and Suren were the happiest people.

Panikkar master led Suren to the waiting Maruti. As they drove through the narrow roads, Mash asked Suren, pointing at the driver,

'Do you recognise him?' Without waiting for Suren's response, Panikkar said, 'This boy is the youngest son of Appunni, you remember, the vegetable seller. Appunni has a double storied house near the high court. Two of his sons are in Saudi. This one is training himself as a driver. Next time his brothers come, they will take him along with them. I am happy for Appunni; his sons have done well.'

Dwarfed between two Dubai mansions, the old-fashioned house of Panikkar master stood patiently, resting its aged body on its antique wooden pillars. Waving at the towering body of the adjoining house, Mash said,

'Prosperity everywhere. Do you see Suren! Lakshmi Amma's two sons are accountants in Dubai. Have a good look at the concrete mansions, built on Dirham power. Who says Free India is not happy and prosperous?'

But nothing had changed inside or outside Mash's house, Suren noted with a strange sense of satisfaction. On the raised platform in the poomukham, sat Mash's old charkha, covered as usual with a tri-coloured cloth—India's national flag.

'Yes, Suren, I still spin one hour in the morning and one hour in the evening. You are surprised at my patience, aren't you? Sitting here, spinning my dreams, has become a way of life with me. You wonder why I am not tired as yet. Well, that is it.'

Suren was amused but not surprised at Mash's uncanny powers of mind reading. Panikkar master was famous for his mesmerising x-ray eyes and the wily way he had with words.

'First, let me light the lamp, and then we will go and see your old friends.' With the burnt end of the matchstick Mash adjusted the flame until it steadied itself to a clear blue and then rubbed the oil-stained hands on his baldpate. Old habits die hard!

Suren watched him quizzically.

Behind Mash's house there used to be an oil mill; the flavour of sesame seeds, sometimes fresh, sometimes stale, when they were thrown away after being pressed, had always added a strange kind of heaviness to the air around his house. Beyond the mill, there were paddy fields. Across the paddy fields, behind the Ganapati temple, on an elevation lived Devayani and her family—her grandmother, mother and her two elder brothers. When her mother became bedridden after a stroke, Devayani had left the school. And she had taken up her mother's job in the temple. Suren had seen her sitting in the outer temple, grinding sandalwood paste on the stone with a pestle and making garlands for the idol. The oil mill had disappeared, so also the paddy fields. In their place, stood a huge building. Mash said that it was a heart-centre, a hospital with all the modern equipment imaginable.'

'Is the Ganapati temple still there? And what about Devayani?'

'Do you think anyone can displace Ganapati? In free India the only way, the best way to ensure a place for yourself is by building a shrine for Mahalakshmi or for Ganapati. No one will dare to evict you. Yes, Devayani still lives there. Devayani was your sister's friend, wasn't she? Then you must know her story?'

'No... Chechi didn't tell me anything.'

'You know Devayani's brothers, what kind of fellows they were. As soon as they managed to find some employment for themselves, they fled their home, leaving the three women to manage for themselves. Devayani worked in the temple, stitched clothes for the neighbours and took care of her mother and grandmother. When the mother died, her brothers came back. Even before the funeral fire had burnt out, they were fighting with their sister for their share in the property. They would have nothing to do with the grandmother. Suren, I must tell you, Devayani gave me the greatest surprise of my life. The way she cut those hen-pecked swine to size! You should have been there to believe it.'

'What property are you talking about? Have you left behind anything to be claimed? This crumbling hovel and the five cents of rocky soil around it – is that what you want? Did it ever occur to you, without a man at home, how we have kept the kitchen fire stirring? You never knew how I had to struggle to make both ends meet. How I managed to buy oils and kashayam for mother? Did you ever think, even once, that you have a sister living here, who needs to be married

off? You have wives, children, jobs and houses. What do I have? After all, I am also a woman What about my needs and desires? Why have you come here now? To light the funeral pyre? Because the scripture says the sons have to do the last rites? Do you think that is the only way to make sure that mother's soul is at peace? I could have lighted the pyre myself. I didn't need your help. After all I am the man *of this house!"*

'Then Devayani had thrown a challenge at them. I was a silent witness, all through. Devayani had specially requested me to be there.'

'I will sign the documents only on one condition; you find a match for me. Your sister is in the thirty-fifth year of her life. Do you know that? Thank your stars, she has not taken to the street; she has not sullied your family name. Like a steady lamp, she has been burning in this house. So you arrange a marriage for her. Do you hear me? Then I will sign the papers.'

'Devayani always had weird ways. For one thing, she felt frustrated with her looks and over the years, toiling for the family, she had hardened herself. Yet, I was surprised at her outburst. The brothers tried all methods, pleading, bribing and even threatening. But Devayani wouldn't budge an inch. Then they started in earnest, looking for a bridegroom for their dear sister. One of their uncles who had migrated to Malabar had a son who was well into his fifties but had not been married for some reason. They brought him over and finally Devayani was married.'

'I must see Devayani,' an odd sense of guilt gnawed at Suren's conscience. Devayani's house stood compact and neat, enclosed within an iron gate. Red brick tiles had replaced the untidy thatched roof. There was no sign of the five-cent compound in which there used to be the one and only mangosteen tree of the town. Suren could never forget those russet brown fruits, Devayani so generously used to distribute in the school. Two thatched houses, a tutorial college and a tailor's shop seemed to have swallowed the compound.

A young girl, about fifteen or so, stood in the front yard, combing her long hair. Suren remembered the girls here never used combs. They didn't believe in 'a hundred rigorous strokes with the brush' which Irene, his wife had recommended to his daughter Jenny. Without a comb, without a brush, with what ease and patience, she separated the knots in her hair! With her bare hands!

'That is Shalini, Devayani's daughter. She is a bright kid. This year she has won a scholarship. She comes to me for help in Maths.'

Shalini just smiled at them. No words of greeting—that was the way here. No *hi*, no *Good day*, not even *namaste*, Suren remembered.

'Is Amma at home?'

Shalini shook her head vigorously in affirmation and went inside to call her mother. Devayani looked changed. There were hardly any warts on her face. She had a healthier, clearer complexion and the middle age bulge had given her a kind of dignity. She was more than pleased to see Suren.

'Oh, Suren, I am so happy! After all these years you have come home! Have you seen my daughter? She wants to become a dancer like your sister. When I see Sharada's photo in the newspaper, I feel so proud.

After all she was my best friend at school. And Mash says you are a great scientist. Had your parents been alive, they would have been so proud!'

'Devayani, do you know why Suren is here? Sharada and he have decided to snap their last link, with our town. Tomorrow morning, he is going to finalise the sale of their tharavade. Do you feel his parents would have been happy?'

'Mash, forget my story. I want to know what Devayani has been doing all these years. Where is your husband, Devayani, why don't you call him?'

'My husband? The last time I had set my eyes on him was thirteen years ago. He left when Shalini was two years old. I tell you, it has been good riddance. He had no job. Just sat at home, eating, drinking and sleeping! In fact, I threw him out. How many mouths could I feed? If I had given birth to a son he might have come back to claim him. A daughter meant only responsibility. So he never showed himself again. Anyway, it is all over and I have no regrets. To tell the truth Suren, what I had just wanted was a child, someone whom I could call my own. He has given me that and I want nothing more. Look at my daughter. Isn't she beautiful? Mash says, she is intelligent. She is working hard for a first class this year.'

Suren couldn't trust his ears. He had not heard a more powerful feminist statement in all his life. He felt a sudden surge of respect for Devayani.

In the morning, Suren hurried with his bath and breakfast. Mash had clearly told him that he must reach the court by nine thirty. They were supposed to meet the dealer first and then the purchasing party. But before that, Suren wanted to have one last glimpse of his ancestral house.

'Suren, you and your sister don't need this house, I know. Sharada's Bangalorean husband and your American wife (not American, Korean, Suren wanted to correct Mash, but he kept quiet) can never settle down here. I understand that. But to me, this house will always remain the tharavade of the Menons. How can I forget the Menons who had taught me the first lessons in patriotism? In the cellars of this house where coconuts and paddy were stored we used to hold our midnight sessions. What heated arguments we used to have—Gandhi, Jinnah, Marx and Lenin ...'

Suren had no ears for the ramblings of Panikkar master. His eyes wandered restlessly around the sprawling house, the mango trees, the gaunt coconut palms bent over the stagnant ponds, the outhouse, the cattleshed and the haystacks, father pacing up and down the front yard, mother plucking jasmine and tulasi... He slowly walked to the backyard and stood before the shrines where his father and mother lay at eternal rest, enclosed in urns, a handful of àsh. He had never lighted a lamp here for them. Even today, he wasn't going to. With his eyes closed, his hands folded, he called out to them to forgive him.

In the court he signed the stamped papers with a shaky hand—I, Surendra Menon, the son of late Velayudha Menon (who was the son of late Shekhara Menon) agree to sell the family house, *Kamalalayam* to the outsider Thomas Tharakan.

Driving back to the railway station, Suren convinced himself, no, consoled himself repeatedly, a trifle sadly, 'I have willingly surrendered and signed away my family heirlooms.'He had to catch the afternoon train, which would directly take him to Bangalore. There he would relieve himself of his video camera and lighten the burden of his bulging suitcase. And next week, he would fly back to J F K. Irene, his wife and Jimmy and Jenny, his children, were sure to be there, waiting for him.

The Garage Sale

Through swirling flakes of snow, as the car turned into Austin Street, he fumbled for the remote and reached for its smooth round luminous centre. The right amount of pressure… the garage, he was sure had responded and lifted her door up without much protest. Last weekend, he had pampered her a lot, oiling and massaging the springs. The remote in the hand gave him a fair amount of power, a vain kind of confidence that he could dictate, control, and bring distances closer.

He turned the key, pushed the door open and peeped in. 'Hi! I am home! Anybody in?'

His voice boomed and came back to him. Apart from the humming of the air-con plant and the swish and starts of the dishwasher, there was absolute silence. The two-legged blackboard, standing in the island of the kitchen, had as many scrawls on it as the space permitted. The round, artistic handwriting of his wife, educated in a convent in the Malabar, stood out against the casual irregular scribble of his daughter and son who went to one of the public schools in Evanston.

'The idlis are wrapped and kept in the microwave. The freshly ground chutney powder is sitting on the table.' Yes, he could smell the punch and pungency of it—asafoetida and chillies. He switched on the exhaust.

Perry would throw a tantrum. He hated the smell of Indian food. If Perry were to be around, Devi could never temper the curries with that extra bit of spice, which he himself was so fond of. You should see Perry, like the pilot of a spaceship armed with mask and headgear, going around the house, dousing curtains and carpets with heavy deodorant sprays! The sticky smell—which was really so very appetising—he said seeped into the pores of his skin and he reeked like a native Indian. As though he was not a native Indian! And Molly, she is allergic to the sandalwood agarbatti which Devi lights, religiously, every morning in their basement shrine. Molly says, the smoke will choke her to death. Sandalwood and spice, the children say, is the *body odour* of every Indian home. What an unkind thing to say!

'I am at Jennifer's. Esther has come down to arrange the garage sale. I am helping her to catalogue Jennifer's stuff.'

Oh yes, he reminded himself, Jennifer, the old dame from the opposite ranch house, his girl friend, as she was widely known, was no more. Her daughter had arrived to take stock of her belongings --- catalogue and fix price tags to her precious stuff. And Devi, his wife was there to assist her.

A day in early August. Jennifer made a desperate call to Kris. The pick-up-van had failed to turn up. She wanted him to drive her over to the soup kitchen. Until a few years ago, without any problem, Jennifer used to drive down to the supermarket and on Sundays, to the church. After the fall she had three winters ago, she had hardly moved out of the house on her own. Esther and George had pleaded with Jennifer to leave the ranch house and go to a condominium. They were willing to keep a nurse-cum -companion for her. Of course, there was no question of Jennifer moving to an Old Home. But Jennifer refused to give in to her children's wish. It was tremendous, the way the septuagenarian stuck to the house built by her late husband and herself, till the very end.

It was a spring morning, Jennifer made him roll down the glass and put her head out to look at the tender green shoots of the maple leaves. The balm of the myrtle that laced the air she said, made her feel fresh, and she breathed in, audibly. She vociferously admired the geraniums and violets, which waved from windows and balconies. She told Kris, again and again, she loved spring. Naturally, in summer and spring she could move around. Fall and winter, she had to confine herself to the house. Problems came, always with winter. In spite of the blowers and electric blankets, she said the cold now seeped into her old brittle bones. She hated the heavy woollens. She complained she felt smothered under their weight. In a light flowery shirt and pistachio green slacks, she looked relaxed, as enthusiastic and eager as a teenager did. Kris looked fondly at her spider-web face, criss-crossed and creased. When the physiotherapist could do nothing about her swollen knees and frozen shoulders, Kris gave her the special herbal oil that he had brought from home on his last visit to India.

It was the special family recipe for arthritis that his mother used to get made at home. Kris remembered, as a little boy, along with the servants, he used to hunt for herbs and roots. He enjoyed hopping around the compound of neighbours, picking leaves and roots. Servants would crush and grind them to a paste and mix it with oil and milk. The concoction would boil for hours in big round brass uruli. With all the authority and knowledge, she had inherited from her ancestors, Amma would supervise the complicated process. It used to be a ritual, sometimes extending to weeks and months. Finally, when the thick blood red thylam was ready, he would help the servants to pour it into bottles and seal them.

Amma treated many of her relations and neighbours who suffered from rheumatism and gout, with the precious concoction. Like mother, like son, he thought as he massaged the oil on Jennifer's aching legs. The oil had miraculously eased Jennifer's knotted joints and she nicknamed it 'Malabar magic'. Kris had become a favourite with Jennifer ever since. Many a Saturday evening or a Sunday afternoon, when Devi would be at a bridal shower, or a baby shower, and the children were at the gym or jogging on the lakefront, he used to sit chatting with Jennifer over gin and beer. Rolling the gin over her tongue, as though it was some precious after-dinner liqueur, she would savour the souvenirs of her bygone days.

'When I talk about the good old days, people shift in their seat and look away awkwardly. What they don't understand Kris, is that I have neither a present nor a future. All I have is a past. You listen to me so very patiently. You pamper me Kris. My own children say I repeat myself and bore them to death, George and Esther have stopped coming down even for Christmas. Last Christmas, I bought a huge turkey and waited for them. At the last minute, they changed their mind and decided to spend Christmas with their friends and finally, I shared the turkey with some old friends in the nursing home.'

Strangely enough, Kris rather enjoyed listening to the stories of the old dame, which always centred on Stephen, her late husband. Perhaps her husband's old connections with the British army, which had taken him to Calcutta and later to Burma, brought him nearer to Kris. The episodes of a tiger hunt and an elephant chase which Jennifer had narrated to him a hundred times, made him feel that Stephen was almost a distant cousin of his. Back home, one of his uncles, a second world war veteran, who had spent a month and a half on the Indo-Burma border, resisting the Japs, had nearly brainwashed him into forgetting the medical profession and enlisting himself in the Indian army. He was never tired of hearing war chronicles.

Jennifer had told him, with fire and frills, the providential escape Stephen and his battalion had from a lone tusker. Some of the soldiers had disturbed a herd of elephants by firing at them at random. All of a sudden, to their horror, a single elephant separated himself from the herd and started chasing them. Ultimately, to protect themselves they had to shoot down the beautiful tusker. The two huge ivory arches of the tusker still stood on the mahogany table, supporting a row of hardcover classics. Next to the table, till recently, had stood the low bookshelf packed with the chocolate coloured gold-rimmed volumes of Encyclopaedia Britannica. Only last month, she had sent them away to the archives. When Jennifer wrote to university libraries, she was willing to give away those treasure-troves of knowledge, all of them declined her generous offer. Of course most politely. Quite understandable. Weren't all encyclopaedias now safely and most economically accommodated in cyberspace? Knowledge was only a mouse-click away! Kris tried in vain to convince Jennifer about the brutal facts of technocracy.

As the car sped past avenues and highways Kris turned quizzically to the old dame. 'Jennifer, why do you insist on going to the soup kitchen? You donate such a huge sum every month - Is that not enough?'

'Oh! Kris, don't you ever talk like George and Esther! Ladling out stew and salad to that hapless crowd, watching them enjoy every bite and every gulp. Don't you think it is much more satisfying than signing away lifeless cheques?'

Hapless! Indeed! Those alchoholics, weirdoes and kleptomaniacs who lined up before the counter and stood clowning around the hall? Kris had no sympathy whatsoever for them. With broken backs and fractured limbs, they were his regular patients in the emergency room. Stitching their heads and putting their limbs together, especially in the Christmas and New Year seasons, had been his routine job. Let Jennifer hobble around the motley crowd and pamper them with a pair of shoes or an overcoat as she was doing now. They would exchange Jennifer's generous gifts for drugs or they would readily sell them for buying booze. There was no doubt about it. Getting into more drunken brawls, sooner or later, they were sure to turn up before him with black eyes and bruises. But Jennifer was totally the mistress of the scene. She would bow before an old man, ruffle the hair of a youngster, and coax someone to eat a little more. What an ecstatic look she had on her face! The glint of Jennifer's irises, a curious blue, stood out against her papery white face, criss-crossed and creased. Kris felt as though he was crystal gazing.

'Unni, take me to the courtyard. After all, I have only a mild fever. I will wrap a shawl around myself. Get me the red kambli with which your father used to cover himself. There...

I feel better. Why? I feel almost fit. Carry an easy chair out. Let me sit and watch them eat. You know the whole village waits eagerly for this event of the year. For the annadanam of Ponmana House, poor folks used to come walking miles and miles from neighbouring villages. I know the boys simply love our milk payasam. Our cook makes it real sweet. The way they lapped it up last year! If the women ask for more pickle, give it to them. Our sour kannimanga is famous in the village. Pregnant women used to crave for them. Give those men more buttermilk. If they are drunk they will straighten up like sticks.' Amma chuckles. That was the last annadanam, Amma had presided.

'Unni, don't pamper her like this. Last night she was shivering under three blankets. As it is, she is asthmatic. If she develops bronchitis, Ponnu and I will have it. You will go away soon. You are not going to be here to take care of her.'

'Do you know how she takes our life out? Thangechi's and mine? Feeding the poor every month, pooja and fireworks in temples all over the country! There is no end to her whims. Unni, you see her only once a year and that too, just for a week!' Ponnechi and Thangechi always reminded Unni, he was only a guest in the house

'She is now planning to give a godanam. People do that only at the time of death. Amma doesn't trust us. That is it.

Don't you think so, Ponnu? She wants to assure her ascent to heaven, holding on to the holy cow's tail! Next, she will ask for a golden calf to be given away as danam. I don't know what sins she is washing away!'

'I know what my sins are, Thangam,. Having carried you and your sister in my womb. Yes, that must have been my sin.'

'Amma, that is enough. Oh! Ponnechi and Thangechi will you stop bullying Amma ?

'Unni, let them talk. They have thousand tongues around their neck.' Amma turns to Thangechi and Ponnechi.

'Lash your tongues at your husbands, those spineless men. Leeches, thriving on our family! They have eyes only for our fields and orchards. Do you think they married you for your looks and brains? Ponmana House, that is what they want. I should have had the courage to give away all my property to some trust, that too, to some Christian trust. But Advocate Pillai quotes rules. In our matriarchal lineage, how can you overlook daughters? What if the daughters are not worthy? Unni, your sisters want the paddy fields and the orchards, all the gold and the silver. If I give you any of those things, they and their husbands would drag you to court. Already a fortune has been spent on you, they grumble, to make you a doctor and to send you to America.' Amma looks around the courtyard and stares at the heap of

mundu and towels.

'Thangam, you haven't got betel leaves and nuts? What if they are not Brahmins? Fold the mundu and the towel and place the betel leaves and nuts on each bundle. That is what we always do. I will hand it over to them. In Ponmana House danam is done in style.'

'Yes Unni, you are the one who has to keep the family traditions alive. I know you are a successful doctor, that too in 'Amerikka.' When Amma grew emotional, she pronounced the word 'America' very proudly with the stress on the 'k' sound as though America was a jathikka, a nutmeg, or a pavakka, a bittergourd!

'Do you know the secret of your success? It is the blessings of Dhanwantara Murthy, our family deity, and of your forefathers. You must continue to have their blessings. That is why I insist you must come down every year in the month of Shravana to hold annadanam in our courtyard. Promise me, you would do that....'

When Jennifer was lying in bed, her right leg in plaster, she went into a brief spell of depression. All because of Esther. Kris tried all his resources—anecdotes, gossip, stories of Indian Gods, the pot-bellied elephant-faced Ganesh—to revive her drooping spirits.

'Who asked you to shuffle around with the vacuum cleaner? You cannot get over your curator's phobia. You and your Persian carpets!' Esther who had come down, cancelling one of her concerts scheduled for the weekend had protested.

Kris could understand Esther's dilemma and he had pleaded on behalf of her. But the old dame took her daughter's words to heart. Kris knew Jennifer looked at the artefacts, she and her husband had collected over the years, with hell of a lot of pride. How possessive she was of the grandfather clock that they had brought along with them all the way from Ireland when they had sailed for New York as immigrants? And the spider lantern bought by her husband in an auction in Venice. The lacquered jewel boxes from Burma, the Baroque style chairs and tables from France, the ornamental mirrors and the coffee tables with their intricate inlays—each one of them enshrined for her a sacred memory. Jennifer had often complained to Kris about her children's indifference. As for Esther, music was the only passion in her life. And in any case, she had no plans to turn her house into a curio shop. Even when Esther was a little girl, she had never been happy with her parents' treasure hunts. Jennifer had confessed to Kris how Esther had given her a jolt once.

'You suffer from a monstrous sense of insecurity, Mamma. Or else, why do you want to hoard things? Tell me Mamma, what are you afraid of?' Rationalising in her own characteristic way, she had literally flung the words at her mother. Hoarding, insecurity, a deep sense of loss, yes, that had been Esther's logistics for her precious stuff! Esther was an ardent student of psychology those days, Jennifer recalled. And she knew her daughter was unkindly referring to her Irish roots. Stephen, who was around, did not attach any importance to Esther's outburst. In fact, he had told her to laugh it off. But she couldn't. She had made up her mind, at once— never to burden her daughter with her *hoarding*.

As for George, he had recently got himself initiated into Buddhism, and worldly treasures had no meaning for him. When he had his whimsical moods of uncertainties and doubts, wondering whether to renounce or to practise an active religion, he ran away to Tibet or Nepal, seeking Rimpoches of a higher order. Finally, Jennifer decided to distribute her artefacts.

On Saturdays, when Kris joined Jennifer for their

gin sessions he sadly watched the slow and steady exodus of the period furniture, chandeliers and crystals. Kris knew Jennifer was almost vengefully cutting herself away, not only from her past but also from life itself. But she was adamant and he could do nothing to dissuade her.

She had asked Kris to take for himself whatever he liked. Somehow he couldn't bring himself to touch any of her treasures. At last, when Jennifer insisted that he must take something from her as a token of love, he had agreed to accept her Bible which, he knew, she was in the habit of reading every day. With the peacock feather, which he himself had presented her once placed as a bookmark on the Book of Job—which rather intrigued Kris – she had left it, specially earmarked for him. After the funeral, Esther had handed it over to him. On the top shelf of his bedroom closet, he had reverentially put it away along with his mother's Ramayanam.

Amma had a rosewood stand, on which she used to keep her Ramayanam open. She would sit cross-legged on the reed mat and read out the verses solemnly, in a tuneful way. She

had never seen the portals of a school. Yet, she could chant full cantos of Bhagavad Gita in chaste Sanskrit. When Amma described the battlefield of Kurukshetra, Kris used to be all ears. Arjuna and Karna. The flying arrows and clashing swords. Agni Astra and Varuna Astra, which rain fire and water around. (What about spit-fires and grenades, bombs and missiles? Kris was almost sure, they must have germinated in the righteous dreams of Amma's Gods.) *Kris didn't much care for the wily Krishna – his namesake – though. And Amma had once punished him for his irreverence. Crossing elbows, holding his ears, he had to touch the ground a hundred and one times. Kris had merrily gone through the feat as though it was a push-up exercise!*

Amma was always worried about the holy books and granthas left by her great grandfathers. They were packed in a large wooden case that looked as big as a small room. Dried neem leaves were scattered above them and they were intact, Kris remembered, when he had passed them on to the Principal of the Ayurveda College.

'Unni, don't think I am not giving you anything. I bequeath to you, all my responsibilities. Our granthas, take good care of them. The mystery of all the herbs and roots – the cure to all the ailments of the world – is inscribed there. And remember tc hold the early festival at the snake shrine. Only a caste Brahmin must do the Ksheerabhishekam.' Last

time he visited India, he had handed over the shrine to the local temple trust. Kris hoped, the abhishekam was being done by a caste Brahmin.

'Do you know, Unni, who built the snake temple? It was built during the time of Rohini Tirunal Maharaja. When a cobra bit the crown prince, all the vaidyas were summoned to the palace. But only our great grandfather could bring down the poison. As a reward, Maharaja had built this shrine for our family.'

With the fourth peg Kris had grown rather groggy-eyed and lethargic. Strange, he felt both heavy and light in the limbs. As though his arms and legs were not his own! He raised his hands and waved them to and fro, to see if they really belonged to him. Like a robot, he propelled himself towards the three-legged blackboard. Perry had scrawled, 'Mom, Jennifer's chess table is for me.' Below her brother's message was Molly's handwriting, all in block letters, 'KEEP ASIDE JENNIFER'S OVAL MIRROR. IT IS FOR ME.'"

Kris picked up the pink crayon and willed his right hand to move across the blackboard. "Prasanna, not Perry, and Malavika not Molly, mark my words; you are not going to take anything from Jennifer. Sridevi, get in touch with the travel agent, we are returning to India.'

Through blurred eyes he peered at the blackboard, and the letters swam in front of him. But his distant vision was getting clearer and more focused. As he threw himself on the bed, popping into his mouth two of those multicoloured magic capsules which he took whenever he got into the mood of packing his bags and taking a flight back home, he could see Amma distinctly. Not as he saw her last, her wizened face inert, spread above the black and green checked blanket. Amma was sitting in front of the kitchen. Tugging at the two ends of the ropes, which were looped around the second toe of her left and right feet, she was churning curds into hillocks of butter. Above the droning of the blower, above the swish and start of the dishwasher, the ropes whirred on, merrily, in musical notes.

'Unni, don't walk in the new rain, you will catch a head cold.' Amma never liked him to get wet in the rain. She always used new rain as an excuse which, she said, brought along

with it all sorts of ailments. Unni always wondered what Amma meant by head cold. He could never find such an ailment in any of his medical dictionaries.

'There, you are walking on the newly dug earth. Don't you step on the earthworms.'

Cutting the long earthworms into bits, was one of the wicked pleasures of Unni, and Amma hated it.

'Wait till you get blisters and rashes on your feet. This time, I will not listen to your pleas. I will set the leeches on you.'

Putting leeches to suck away impurities, was one of Amma's famous treatments for which people came from the length and breadth of the country. Kris could hear Amma singing her favourite song.

'Come, my Unnikrishna!
I will roll for you, a big ball of butter.
Anatbalayolam venna tharameda,
Ananda Shrikrisna, vaa thurakke.
I will give you butter, as big as an elephant's head,
Open your mouth, my little Krishna'

Amma was not Yashoda, Lord Krishna's mother, who begged her son to close his mouth lest she faint. She had only asked Unni to open his mouth so that she could feed him. And, after all, Unni was only a mortal Unnikrishna. Unlike Lord Krishna, he didn't hold in his mouth, heaven or hell, continents or oceans to ward his mother off! Yet...

Hide and Seek

Daintily picking up the hem of her flowing skirt, Mini bent down on her knees and slid into the gap between the sideboard and the wall. There was just enough space for her to squat. If she felt too stiff she could raise her knees. Spiders and cockroaches were not likely to cross her way here. She need not have any fear on that score. Grandmother kept the sideboard spotlessly clean. She dusted its sides, the legs and the top daily and wiped it clean with a soft white towel. She would hold the towel against the sun and examine it minutely to see how much dust had come off. With lemon peels and tamarind pulp, she scrubbed the fan-shaped brass knobs of the drawers until they stood against the dark background of rosewood, shiny and smooth.

The sideboard belonged to grandfather who was no more. Grandfather had worked on a rubber estate with a white man for a boss. When the white man returned to his own country for good, he left the sideboard behind as a farewell gift for grandpa. Grandpa kept all his important papers, his money and even grandma's jewellery in those drawers, which were still kept under lock and key. On the finely polished top, stood grandfather's betel box, a cute casket in rosewood. Grandmother looked at the sideboard with love and respect as though she was looking at grandfather himself. When grandmother was in one of her generous moods, she would allow Mini to open the precious box and view the silver miniatures of clove and cardamom that were kept wrapped in cotton pads in one of the inner compartments. On rare occasions, when she was allowed to hold the tiny treasures in her palms, Mini felt important and honoured.

Come to think of it, the antique sideboard was an odd piece in their otherwise sparsely furnished home. Father's office room had a row of rusty, rickety chairs where his clients sat waiting for their turn. Father sat behind a square table covered with a dull grey plastic sheet, peering into files and folders. Babu, the boy next door, once told her that those who came to see her father, were cheats and criminals. What a fight she had had with him! His father was a doctor, who gave a fresh lease of life to people. So Babu claimed. But he had no right to talk about her father in such mean terms. When Mini told Father all about it, he only laughed. 'Tell Babu, if I don't take care of those scoundrels, his father will be unable to go on his rounds peacefully,' he said. Those fat books, which were kept in dusty piles in the cupboard, father told her, were about rules and laws to keep people out of mischief. Mini found those books with their ugly black leather covers, a big bore. No stories, no colour pictures. Mini decided she would have nothing to do with such books.

She looked down admiringly at the billowy spread of her silk skirt. Almost for the hundredth time, with her tiny fingers, she felt the softness of the rich material. A silk skirt with a brilliant brocade border. With great pride, she caressed the tiny gold stars woven into its body. What a contrast to those coarse knee-length cotton frocks which she was normally made to wear! Grandma would not allow her to wear skirts. What if she tripped and fell? There was no end to grandma's worries. But today, as she stepped into her new skirt, even grandma was all smiles. It was an auspicious day, and a suitable dress for the occasion, was a matter of right for Mini.

The house was full of people. Mini strained her ears to listen to the voices in the house. She never knew she had so many aunts, uncles and cousins! All those aunts were wearing such heavy and shining jewellery! Each one of them hugged her and made it a point to pinch her on her cheeks. She knew she had beautiful cheeks. Her father said they were like two roses. But she did not want to be pecked and smothered by those fat aunts!

All the same, she kept a smiling face. She remembered Grandma had pleaded with her not to fight with anyone. For the last one week, Grandma had been so preoccupied. So busy looking after the visitors that she had almost forgotten Mini. Would you believe it, today she had not remembered to give Mini her oatmeal and vitamins? Not that she minded it. She hated the sticky porridge. And how many times had she pried those multicoloured capsules open, just to look at the sticky substance inside! But of course, she would always make sure that Grandma was nowhere around... Poor Grandma! She was so patient with her. She could never bring herself to punish her little darling.

In fact, it was Mini who gave her a tough time. Grandma just had to refuse her a ribbon or a hair clip and Mini would bring the house down. Grandma thought girls looked beautiful with long hair. But father didn't agree. The barber who came home to cut father's hair took pains to give Mini a trendy haircut. But Grandma never approved. Struggling with bows and bands, she would grumble and protest. If Mini had long hair, she could have easily plaited it. But all these fashions, she said, were beyond her. It was high time Mini got a mother. She would sigh and look at her son imploringly. Once the dinner was over, as Mini lay dozing on her lap, Grandma would launch upon her litany. She would talk softly to her son about Mini's future, how important it was that she should have a young woman to take care of her. Not this old lady who was in the evening of her life. When requests and pleadings would fail to move father, she would resort to threats and even, blackmail. Listening to father's counter arguments, Mini would fall asleep.

Sometimes Mini felt that Grandma was right. She had no memory of her mother. When Grandma took her along to the temple, the ladies from the neighbourhood would stop and look at her with sorrowful eyes. ' Look at the sharp nose, those big eyes, the same complexion! She is a carbon copy of Tara.' Mini wondered why they sounded so regretful. Her mother might have been beautiful. But to have a mother frozen within a photo frame did not help her in anyway. Why did she have to be called by God? Mini could not understand. When the old coconut tree fell, father said, death came with old age. But her mother had not been old!

Mini remembered the day she had gone for the

birthday party of Sindhu, her best friend. Sindhu's house was so beautifully decorated. It almost took her breath away. Festoons and balloons hung from the ceiling in criss-cross patterns. There were flowers in every nook and corner. As Sindhu and her mother came and took her in, she felt she was walking into heaven. So bright and colourful!

How beautiful Sindhu's mother was! She buzzed around the hall like a bee. She even played hide and seek with them. If she asked grandma to play with her, she would start her usual complaints. There was always some thing wrong with her knees, or legs, or arms. Look at Sindhu's mother. She could run so fast! Mini managed to catch her only because she had allowed herself to be caught. When she was led to the table where the snacks were arranged she was surprised. She didn't know there could be sweetmeats in such shapes and colours. Grandma could only make black and white balls of semolina laced with coconut and jaggery. At the centre of the table, stood a huge cake with five tiny candles glowing on it. When she watched Sindhu blowing them off in a single breath, she was thrilled! How delicious the cake was!

When grandma told her that her father was going to bring home a young bride who was going to be her new mother, Mini was overjoyed. For days, she could think and talk of nothing else but her new mother. Like Sindhu's mother, her mother too would turn her home into a heaven. She had already planned she would call all her friends home. Let them know she also had a mother.

As the big day dawned, the house wore a festive look. Uncles and aunts, neighbours and friends, were moving in and out of the house. When father got into the car with the aunts, Mini, dressed in all her finery, naturally followed him. But grandma pulled her back. 'Let them go, both of us will stay back,' she said. How could that be? Mini turned to her father for support. But what a surprise! He said nothing at all. How could her father be so heartless? As the car moved out of sight she burst into tears.

'They have to go a long way. Don't you remember, last time when we went to town, how sick you felt? You hated the long ride. I know the smell of petrol is too strong. It gives you nausea. I am not going either. There is so much to do! Remind me to order for flowers and banana leaves. We have to arrange the hall and the rooms. They will be here in no time. We will stand at the gate to welcome your new mother.' Grandma kissed her tears away and assured her. Mini was not convinced. Yet, she wouldn't throw any tantrums. After all, in a while she would have her mother by her side. Hours dragged by. How long could she sit inside waiting for them to arrive!

Across the fence, she could see Babu. Oh yes! She would tell Babu how happy, how excited she was. Crossing the fence, she ran into Babu's garden. As usual, he was running up and down, trying to catch Grandpa's beard, the flying cottonseeds. Why didn't Babu turn to look at her? Was she not looking pretty? Wasn't her skirt beautiful? 'Are you not happy I am going to have a new mother?' Holding her skirt above the ground, she whirled round and round and chirped.

'Don't you know, the new mother will only be a stepmother to you? All stepmothers are cruel. I know it. She won't love you. I feel sorry for you.'

With all the wisdom of a seven-year-old, Babu faced her. Of course, she knew Babu was full two years older than she was. And wasn't he clever? How she envied him! Certainly, he knew a lot more than she did. Could he be right? What could he mean by stepmother? In those fairy tales father read out to her, she had come across stepmothers. Yes, Babu was right, stepmothers *were* always cruel. They punished children, starved them and made them slog. What if her new mother turned out to be a witch? No, no! She could not take it anymore. She ran all the way back to the south wing of the house. She knew where to hide. Grandma's giant sideboard. It would shield her. She didn't want to see anyone, not even the new mother.

Mini woke up with a start. Propped against the wall, her knees resting on the sideboard, she had fallen asleep. How long had she been there? She remembered she had come running straight from Babu's home, all the way to the shelter of the sideboard and she had cried herself to sleep. Stiff and numb in her limbs, she stretched her legs as far as she could and peeped out. No sign of anyone. Come what may, she would not budge an inch out of her hiding place. No one would dream of looking for her here. Let Grandma comb the length and breadth of the house. Let her puff and pant, and peer into all the lofts and all the cellars of the house. Mini couldn't care less.

What a disaster! She could hear footsteps. Surely, someone was coming. Oh! It was Grandma and she was calling out to her. There was someone else with her. Was it not her father's voice? They seem to be looking for Mini frantically. It served them right. Who was it now? Was it not Sundari who was purring? How could she get here? Sniffing and pawing she had almost reached the sideboard. Did she smell a rat behind? There she was. How clever! Sundari stood there, triumphantly looking straight at Mini with her green eyes. With one leap, she landed on Mini's lap like a snow-white ball, furry and soft. Why did Sundari have to expose her? She could see Grandma's arms reaching out to her.

As Grandma pulled her out and put her on her feet, she looked around. Oh! God! The room was full of people. So many faces! Worried and anxious, all turned towards her. It was so scary. She kept her eyes down. A pair of black leather shoes, brand new and shiny, creaked across the floor. Mini knew, for sure, it was father. He was coming closer. Behind him, she could see a pair of feet, delicate and fair. The silver anklets on them tinkled intriguingly. That must be her mother. She wouldn't look at her. As father lifted her up, she closed her eyes tight and covered her face with both hands. She could feel a pair of hands on her shoulders. Someone was trying to take her from her father. The touch was feather-like. So very gentle!

As mother hugged Mini to her bosom, she could feel the softness of the material she wore and hear the 'tick-tick' of her heartbeats. Was mother also worried? Just as Mini was? The breath on Mini's cheeks was warm and balmy, as though the fragrance of all the flowers in the garden had blended in. As she tried to pull the little hands away from her face, Mini had a glimpse of her mother. Her face was bright and round like the full moon that rose behind the cocoa tree in the backyard. Wasn't she beautiful? Even more beautiful than Sindhu's mother! She didn't look harsh at all. Not even a little bit! She couldn't be cruel. Babu need not always be right. Her mother was going to love her. Yes, she felt almost sure. As she locked her arms around her mother's neck, she saw her father heave a sigh of relief. Father grinned, Grandma smiled, aunts and uncles, cousins and friends who crowded around the hall, beamed at her, and Mini hid her head shyly on her mother's shoulders.

Kunji Kutti

Asylums were not very common those days. Moreover, a person like Kunji Kutti could ill-afford such a luxury. She had no one, dear or near. Who would have wished to bring Kunji Kutti, the mad woman, back to sanity? For love, for charity or even for a challenge? No. No one would have taken upon himself or herself such an unrewarding task. A reject, a destitute, she lived outside the two-acre temple ground, under the old banyan tree, the sacred age-old banyan tree of the village. A slate-grey cement slab, about two feet high and four feet wide, ran around the base of the tree, furnishing Kunji Kutti with a roomy open-air apartment.

Anyone who walked into the temple ground, could have a full view of Kunji Kutti's home which looked more or less like a stage in an amphitheatre. On the side, facing the temple, she stocked her pots and pans and on the other side, she kept a pile of firewood—twigs and branches of all sorts tied in neat bundles. At the root of the banyan tree she kept an earthen lamp which she lighted religiously at the break of dawn and at the fall of dusk. One of the hollows hidden in the trunk of the tree served her as a shelf where she kept all her treasures- cowrie shells, peacock feathers, pink and green glossy sheets of paper, publicity pamphlets thrown around by the local cinema house to promote their latest arrivals.

Was she born crazy? Was she driven to madness? Had some unforeseen event --- a tragedy in the family or an accident--- thrown her off her balance? No one ever knew. For ages, she had been living under the old banyan tree. How old was she? Not very old. Could have been in her late thirties. The tattered, soiled clothes she wore could hardly conceal her full, buxom figure. The village women, as they walked past the banyan tree on their way to the temple, looked at her with embarrassment. They might have been jealous of her or they were afraid of her for some vague reasons. They readily donated jackets and dhotis to her, lest their husbands, brothers or sons went wayward.

Her ear lobes, which were pricked to accommodate, perhaps at some time, large-sized studs, were now naked and hung loose in saggy, boat-like slits. Into those slits she shoved in flowers, huge hibiscus, pink and red, wild berries or at times long blades of grass. She had short curly hair, not bobbed, not cut to shape, but chopped above her shoulders. It was very unusual those days, for women to have short hair. Most village women wore their hair in glossy buns, which rested on the nape of their neck or let their hair loose which came cascading down their ample backs. Westernised women, very old women or invalids had their hair cut. Perhaps, Kunji Kutti qualified for the last category. She was a mentally ill person. Afternoons, she would sit by the side of the slimy pool and comb her curls with wet fingers. She carefully picked lice from her head and with great relish squashed those squirmy swollen creatures between her nails and wiped the blood off on the grass.

There were three temples in the village. The Krishna temple with Bala Murali as its idol, was the most popular even in those days. None of us would ever miss the evening deeparadhana. The temple priest must have been an artist of sorts. After the evening pooja, as the doors of the inner shrine were thrown open, Krishna—painted gold and yellow in sandalwood and turmeric paste, his eyes and brows accentuated in black kohl, resplendent with jewels and garlands—would look smilingly at the devotees. Conches are blown even today, but never so loud, never so solemn! The brass bells clanged continuously and camphor and incense hung heavily in the air. Some of us swooned and some were moved to ecstatic tears. Beating their breast they would chant in chorus 'Hare

Krishna, Hare Krishna.'

The devi temples of Kali and Lakshmi also attracted a large number of people. The most colourful and the most awaited event of the village calendar was the Utsavam, the yearly festival of these three temples. Men, women and children thronged the temple ground to participate in the festivities. Special pandals were erected where maestros conducted concerts of vocal and instrumental music. All night there would be Kathakali performances, rendering of classics like *'Nala charitam'* or *'Kuchela Vritbam'*.

The most unique feature of our utsavam, those days, was the concluding event, the confluence or rather, the conference of the three deities. The idols, Krishna flanked by the two Devis, sat on decorated elephants beneath crimson and gold canopies made of the finest silk. Comforted and cajoled by feather fans, swaying rhythmically to the beat of the drums, the Gods would nod or vigorously shake their heads. We stood in awe and watched them intently. A nod meant approval. We were elated. While an angry jerk, a dissent obviously meant something was wrong. It alarmed us. The nadaswaram would at once take a pleading note and repeat the pallavi and the anupallavi. And the drums would boom louder and louder. A desperate attempt to appease the Gods! Finally, they would bow and take leave of each other, with the silent promise that they would meet again next year.

Kunji Kutti made herself conspicuous in the Utsavam crowd. As the fireworks, the finale of the ritual, broke out, she would jump down the parapet where she had been sitting and would go spinning round and round on the gravelled ground, like a top. She muttered unintelligible words and those who stood watching her commented that the evil spirits which had enslaved her mind and body, were probably being chased away.

The next morning, in front of the local government school, Kunji Kutti, to the delight of the school children, enacted the temple scenes. She would pose as a lovelorn Damayanti, coyly receiving messages from the stately swans, or as a humble Kuchela who looked beseechingly at Krishna as he took a mouthful of puffed rice. She sang, she danced, she laughed, she cried and the children broke into peals and peals of laughter. They paid Kunji Kutti for the entertainment with the crescent-shaped candies that they had bought at the sweet vendor's. The truck driver, who brought the mid-day meal for the school children, always remembered to give her a share of the rice gruel.

In front of the school building, during the long interval for lunch, there was always a motley crowd. Karim, the bangle seller, in his striped lungi with a colourful scarf tied around his head, sat on the ground with a box full of bangles, multi-coloured glass and plastic bangles. He also had ribbons and funny fibre-like false hair switches, which he kept suspended from a pole near the box. The bangle corner was the haunt of teenage girls. Karim lovingly accepted the outstretched hands of the girls. As he slipped the rainbow-coloured tinkling glass bangles on to their wrist, he would innocently squeeze and pinch those slender, shapely arms. God only knew from where, but Kunji Kutti would come charging down, grimacing at Karim all the way, and throw at him a spider or a frog which she kept hidden in her bundle to scare people off.

The village had two big houses, one belonged to the chief priest of the temple and the other to the Raja. Though he was called Raja, he was not really a king. He belonged to the family of the rulers of yesteryears and Raja was now only a kind of surname for him. Kunji Kutti visited these two houses regularly for her quota of rice, pulses and vegetables.

Twice a year, during harvest time, she would go to

the Raja for her measure of rice. She wandered around the mansion of the Raja and stealthily picked up a coconut, or swiped a handful of tamarind from the mat where it was spread out to dry. Kannan, the caretaker of the house, so conscientious and alert, would go chasing her, to retrieve the pilfered goods. When she knew she was really caught, she would abruptly stop in her track. She stood like a statue rooted to the ground, and giggled.

From the corner of her eyes, she wryly watched the widowed sister of the Raja who sat on the veranda, stringing together jasmine and tulsi into a garland for the family deity. She was a pale, puny creature, always ready to fade into the background. Kunji Kutti tapped the coconut as though it were a drum and declared in a comically singsong voice, 'Oh you saw me picking the coconut! I saw you. Behind the cowshed. On the hayloft. You were with someone.' She threw another sidelong glance at the devout lady on the veranda. The pale creature grew paler and hastily disappeared into the inner chambers and Kannan discreetly retreated to the backyard. After all, he had to supervise the threshing. Without a care in the world, Kunji Kutti stood her own ground, and continued to giggle like an idiot.

The priest owned the biggest matham in our village. You know how mathams are— the inner rooms built in a row, connected like compartments in a train. His mother, a stern-faced widow, her shaven head tightly covered with the loose end of her coarse white sari, would stand like a sentinel in their barred veranda. She never stepped out of her house. Yet, she was a terror in the village. If the shadow of a human form crossed their courtyard, she would yell in her treble shrill voice. Her daughter-in-law would promptly come out with a shining brass pitcher and sprinkle holy water around. To purify the defiled air and space invaded by lesser beings!

Our Kunji Kutti, of course, feared no mortal on earth. She would stealthily creep close to the bars and phoo...phooo the stooping lady, and startle her out of her vigil. The lady used the choicest curses on poor Kunji Kutti, reserved usually, for a woman of the street. But nothing could rattle Kunji Kutti. Making devilish faces at the two women, she would run around the entire compound and call out to them to fetch holy water. Finally, as she collected her quota of temple prasadam, she would stare solemnly at the young woman, at her bejewelled nose, her shimmering necklace, bracelets and anklets. And then she would break out sighing and moaning for the stolen property of the temple! A couple of years ago, we had a major theft in our Krishna temple. The rubies and emeralds, the gold ornaments and the silver items mysteriously disappeared from the inner shrine. Though the thieves were caught, it had caused quite a stir in our quiet village.

'Let lightning strike them, let vipers sting them, let them be roasted alive. How dare they take the jewels off the idol? Fetch cauldrons full of Ganga jal. You must wash the temple,' she would burst out in a fit of fury. Passing her sanest strictures on all sinners, priest or no priest, she would walk out, leaving behind her, her nonplussed audience, the mother-in-law and the daughter-in-law.

That was the first general election after the death of Pandit Nehru. There were so many political parties and so many contestants! There were candidates from every walk of life. We didn't know whom to choose – the Raja's son, the Priest's son, the Headmaster's wife – were all well into the fray. I remember distinctly, it was an unusually eventful election. We were surprised when a distiller from our neighbourhood became, almost overnight, politically ambitious. We were told that he had support from distant Delhi. He promised us more schools, more electricity, more water, if we elected him to power. He sincerely wished and vowed to put our humble unknown village on the big map of India. He set *task forces* and *time frames* and involved us in hectic activities. Roads were cleared and garbage was burnt. Beggars were chased away, stray dogs were rounded up, and Kunji Kutti the mad woman disappeared.

Some people say she went underground to evade the over enthusiastic volunteers. Some say, she had been sent away to an asylum. In any case, she never came back to our village. Has she found another banyan tree, in another village? Is she languishing in the narrow cells of a faraway madhouse? Or, has she lost herself in the back streets of some filthy city? We wonder. We still talk to our children about Kunji Kutti. As we walk past the banyan tree to the temple grounds, we wish she were still there. But the banyan tree has now become a base of the local rowdies. No young woman can walk past without embarrassment, without being exposed to a microscopic scrutiny.

The Socialite

We called her Titli. We knew it was not her real name. We didn't bother to find out how she signed her letters or cheques. Why should we? The name sat pretty and perfect on her— fitting her like a glove. Our Titli was really a titli, a butterfly, cute and colourful, flitting in and out, up and down our social orbit. Not that she hopped from flower to flower seeking nectar or any such thing. Far from it. When her eagle-eyed husband winged his way across foreign skies promoting and consolidating his ambitious business projects, she dutifully waited for him, holding the fort at home. Of course, she had her own close friends like me, with whom she went circling round shopping malls, hunting for bone china, cosmetics and the latest dress material.

I don't know what made her befriend me. As an underpaid university teacher, I had neither the riches nor the glamour to attract a popular socialite like Titli. But the day I first met her – it was at a diplomatic function – she took to me with a kind of pathetic persistence. Later on, she told me it was my name that attracted her first. Shama was as unique and wistful a name as Titli. She had no idea my real name was Shyamoli, aptly given, so I was told, for my swarthy complexion. When the Chinks and Yankees around me found my name a tongue twister, I readily accepted the name they gave me. But Titli's imagination indulged me. To her, I was like one of those *consuming shamas* enshrined in an Urdu ghazal. And I, for my part, found the romantic streak in her personality absolutely charming.

Once, I had overheard one of the senior members of the expatriate community contemptuously describing Titli's meteoric rise in our *partying* circle, how from a plain Jane she had emerged as a *hep* chic.

'Don't I remember Mandy as the simple Mandeep?' Mrs. Yogi ravenously went over the details... 'You should have seen Mandeep, operating from an apartment in the suburbs! A petty garment trader, struggling to make both ends meet. Knocking around. Door to door!'

She travelled further back in time and narrated to a rapt audience, how Mandeep's widowed aunt had fought tooth and nail with the immigration office to get him to the U.S. Ultimately, Jessie —Mandy's aunt— one of the dedicated Florence Nightingales who came to this country, crossing oceans and scaling clouds to light the lamp for the sick and for their own families back home, had to adopt Mandy to wangle a green card for him. As he graduated to the more respectable business of building and construction, he imported from the homeland, a genuinely desi bride for himself.

Mandy took her straight to Madam Reena's beauty salon. Her waist-length wispy hair was ruthlessly scissored above the shoulders. Treated with chemicals and permed to perfection, her hair now hung in coils around her head. Madam Reena taught her how to walk on stilettos, to speak English with a drawl and to choose her wardrobe and the plain Jane soon emerged as a suave socialite. It was an intriguing coincidence that as Titli came out of the finishing school of Madam Reena, Mandy's fortune took quantum leaps. Contracts came pouring Mandy's way and Mrs. Yogi knew pretty well who was behind Mandy's success. Certainly not Dame Luck but Dame Titli.

Titli had confessed to me once or twice, how she had loathed—initially—attending parties and felicitating and favouring the commercial bigwigs. But Mandy had convinced her it was absolutely necessary for business promotion. And Titli had reluctantly given in to her husband's wish. After all she was a devoted wife.

'Now we see her splashed across the society pages in newspapers, gracing charity shows, chairing committees, cutting ribbons—inaugurating fashion shows and art shows! 'Mrs. Yogi droned on. If her voice was laced with venom, didn't I know the reason for it?

When Bhaktananda, the godman of our century visited the city, Mrs. Yogi had taken it for granted he would camp in her house. After all, Dr. Yogi was indisputably, the most senior and the most prosperous member of the expatriate community. A successful cosmetic surgeon in the city, Dr. Yogi's clientele extended far beyond, to the neighbouring states. Mrs. Yogi's palatial house, replete with spacious lawns, swimming pools, and with white hibiscus and red-stemmed palms shipped all the way from South East Asia, would certainly have been the most suitable sanctuary for the holy man.

When the association of the local followers of Bhaktananda unanimously chose Titli's house as a venue for the holy meet, it did not just shock Mrs. Yogi. It infuriated her. Titli, the simple soul as she was, never took it as a triumph to gloat over-least of all over Mrs. Yogi. But characteristically enough, Mrs. Yogi could not forget and forgive. She missed no chance--- ever since--- to humiliate Mandy and Titli in public by harping on his humble beginnings and her behenji background.

I was quite surprised when she took to inviting me for her exclusive coffee mornings. In the high profile society where people like Mrs. Yogi consciously held their sway, a poor teacher like me was a nonentity. But soon, I could sense the reasons for her new-found interest in me. Every time she referred to the meanness of Mandy and the pettiness of Titli, she would casually throw a glance at me. Obviously, she wanted to ensure that I carried the tales to Titli. She was so confident that Titli would mess up the arrangements for the visit of the holy man, that she threw a challenge to her fans. She had a two hundred-dollar bet with one of them that the whole thing would turn into a fiasco. But Titli gave Mrs. Yogi the surprise of her life. In spite of her wicked prayers and evil wishes, Titli made the sacred visit a memorable event.

She didn't have spacious lawns like Mrs. Yogi to accommodate the flow of the devotees. From the length and breath of the country, people kept pouring in—the white, the black, the brown and the yellow - all folks, young and old eager to have darshan of Swamiji. I must admire my dear friend's resourcefulness. With what ingenuity she turned her basement into a temple -- a veritable high-tech temple. Through well-distributed ducts, the temperature of the basement was maintained cool or warm, in tune with the whims of the October weather. The lighting was brilliantly manipulated. Oil lamps, fluorescent bulbs, candles, multicoloured -- everything contributed to the mystique of the temple. Atop the hill, hewn out of plaster of Paris, Gods and Goddesses stood, appropriately mounted on their respective vahanas. Concealed speakers periodically chanted *Om* and electrified the air.

It was an experience of a lifetime for the local crowd. For hours, they hovered around the miniature idols, drinking in the minutest detail -- the deadly snakes coiled around the blue-stained neck of Shiva, the tiny veena of Saraswati, the reed flute of Krishna, the resplendent Shri Chakra of Vishnu. The ultimate, was the alcove in the corner. That was my brainchild. I never knew that the in-house decorators of the Imperial Hotel would be able to furnish us with such a fantastic ice sculpture. Those who walked into the alcove almost swooned at the sight of the well-chiselled, translucent Shivaling cast in ice. Many people thought it was meant to be the replica of the reputed cave of Amarnath. We had not planned anything as ambitious. But when people raved about the evident ingenuity and artistic prowess, we were thrilled. I saw Mrs. Yogi prowling around the alcove with a scowl on her face. After all, Titli had won hands down and Mrs. Yogi could only lick her wounds and wait.

Imagine, once again Mandy and Titli have been honoured. Today the cultural delegation from India on a goodwill visit to the U. S., is scheduled to meet in Titli's house. Titli was a little nervous about this party. A religious meet is one thing but a cultural meet is altogether a different story. She had insisted that I supervise all the arrangements and be with her until the last guest departed. Mrs. Yogi had more then once hinted, well in my presence, that Titli's devotion to me was not all that selfless. She was patronising me so that I would fill gaps for her, so said Mrs. Yogi. Of course, I helped her to plan her parties and at times even told her how to make conversation. But I thoroughly enjoyed doing all that. There was no question of Titli and Mandy exploiting me. What nonsense!

I looked at the checklist for the hundredth time. Every fresh arrival was tallied with the guest list. We didn't want any gatecrashers and couldn't afford to take any risk with the security of the dignitaries. The delegation represented people from every walk of life—political leaders, social workers, artists and women activists—it was a well-balanced group. And the local crowd was equally balanced. Imtiaz the crooner, the permanent entertainer at Titli's parties had come armed with his latest mix-n-match tunes. But I thought it would be wiser to play some real classy music. Thumris, ghazals, Ravi Shankar and Chitti Babu, conjured up an ideal ambience for cultural exchange.

Liquor was not in my jurisdiction. But I saw the bartenders wringing their hands in exasperation. They couldn't have a moment of respite. Mandy had arranged a more than generous amount of drinks, a variety of them. Swish... clink... clank... glasses were filled. Ice-cubes tinkled. Cheering, toasting, guffawing, and whispering, the cultural party, I could see, was in full swing.

One of the elderly guests—I remember, he was introduced to us as a freedom fighter who had spent the prime years of his life in political prisons—had settled himself in the s-shaped sofa, the lover's seat, as it was called. He was humming rather tunelessly to himself with the background music of Jagit-Chitra, longing for the glory of childhood....

Woh kagaz ki kashti woh baarish kaa paani...

I looked at him with fascination. He was twisting and turning the round shaped bronze coloured buttons on the back rest of the sofa as though he would exchange anything to get back the glories of bygone days. I knew he would soon fall asleep. I made a mental note, to warn Mandy lest the cultural delegation leave him behind. I could hear the rich sophisticatedly modulated voice of Mary, distinctly above the clamour. She was the chairperson of ChildHome, one of the reputed charity homes of the city.

'Give us the details of those orphanages. We Americans will do any thing to wipe the tears of these unfortunate children. Medicines, food, clothes. Just name it. We will organise how to send them across.'

The women activists were nodding their heads attentively and taking notes solemnly. One among them, in a Rajasthani outfit, was animatedly looking at Mary's golden bracelet, the amulets, tiny toads, scorpions and snakes, dangling from the delicate chain on her slim wrist. At last, she plucked enough courage to ask Mary from where she had brought it. Soon, there was a vociferous exchange of notes among them about the price of gold and the availability of genuine corals and jades. Mary had by now caught hold of Titli. Savouring the succulent coils of jalebi, she was pleading with Titli to hold a demonstration of the intricacies of the Indian sweets in her house.

Mandy was taking some of the distinguished men on a conducted tour through halls and corridors. With a duly impressed crowd, he had now stopped in front of a figurine – an old bearded man, balancing a faggot on his shoulders.

'Have a look. Solid wood. And you know, it is carved out of a single piece. No joints, no pasting. Feel the texture with your own hands. Isn't it smooth? Only a master craftsman can manage to get such perfection.'

I had a tough time controlling my laughter. Titli had once told me how she had come up on this artistic marvel in one of the back streets of Old Delhi. She said she had thoroughly enjoyed herself, bargaining with the Banjara woman on the footpath. Finally, she had bought it from the poor woman for a ridiculously low price! Were there no connoisseurs around, who could expose Mandy?

One of his American guests was complimenting him on his excellent choice of carpets. The carpet on which they stood was really, a classic one. The geometrical patterns in delicate muted colours were interwoven very skilfully. 'The number of knots you know, that is what tells the quality of a carpet...' Mandy was obviously trying to show off his professional knowledge. A sharp screeching sound... Oh! A young man dressed casually in a loose kurta and pajama had pushed his chair off. Running his fingers through his flowing beard he was staring at Mandy. Strange! Why was he charging towards Mandy?

'How dare you man! How dare you gloat over your Goddamned artefacts? How many young boys must have given their blood to colour your carpets? Knots indeed! Those tiny fingers, which have tied them, do you remember them?'

Wow, what courage! What commitment! I looked at him carefully. The glass in his hand, the brown liquid, was it Coke or rum?

As I was seriously debating the question, I caught sight of Mrs. Yogi. What was she doing at the bar? I must keep a close watch. Mrs. Yogi was in close conference with the bartenders. I saw her pointing out to the far end of the hall. Perhaps, she was asking him to take a drink to someone special. I must follow the attendant. Oh God! Titli had taken the goblet from him!

What calamity were we in for? I tried desperately to reach my friend. It was tantalising. Every time I managed to get near her, someone or the other intercepted either her or me. And I watched in alarm as Titli drained the goblet to the last drop.

By the time I got through the crowd to Titli, she was standing in front of the freedom fighter, who had curled himself to sleep on the S-sofa. Titli called out to him in a silky voice. Coming out of his fitful sleep, he scrambled out of the sofa and stood blinking at her. Titli snatched a glass from an attender who was passing by. Oh! I must stop her.

'Uncle, You must have a drink. It is the world's best brandy. Cognac from the South of France. You shouldn't miss it.'

He turned away from her, with his hands tightly closed over his mouth. A striking posture, like the legendary painting of Ravi Varma which graced the wall of Titli's living room. The divinely beautiful Menaka pleading with the furious Saint Vishwamitra— the famous betrayal scene.

'Oh! You can't say no to me. Don't try to resist me. How can you? Do you know who I am? Do you know what is my name? My name is Tilottama...'

Oh! I can never forget the stupefied expression on

the face of the poor old man. Was it really Titli who was speaking? Did I hear her right? Was I tipsy? How could that be? I had not taken even a drop of alcohol! I watched Titli helplessly. Raising herself on her heels, she was swaying, back and forth. And she looked so seductive!

'I am Tilottama, the apsara from Indra's court. Who can resist me?'

By the time I reached Titli, a large crowd, including Mrs. Yogi had formed a formidable horseshoe formation around her. As I caught my dear friend in my arms, firmly ignoring the sniggers, she blacked out. Most mercifully. At last, pushing his way through the crowd, Mandy came. And I quietly handed Titli over to him.

A Distant Summer

The two lions, crudely shaped, sat on either side of the gate glaring at each other. With scruffy fingers, feeling the rib-like mane of those cement lions, I used to sit on the high wall, waiting for the old school master. I couldn't really say I was waiting. I always wished he didn't come. But I knew he would always come. The soft green mounds of moss, which grew in erratic patterns on the crevices of the aged wall, lashed by rain and eroded by the sun, were fascinating. Scooping a handful of the powdery moss and spilling it around and squinting against the rising sun, I would keep my eastward-watch.

As punctual as the rising sun, he would appear on the eastern bend of the narrow road, the russet, ribbon-like strip of a road which went winding down to the east fort of the town. A tall, lean man, he walked with measured strides, briskly for all his three score years. Under his right arm, he carried his greying umbrella with its hateful hooded end with which he would jerk me off my perch of surveillance.

There were never any words of greeting. Neither from him, nor from me. With books, slate and the freshly plucked cactus – its juicy sap served me as an eraser – I would run ahead of him to the outhouse, to its open corridor flanked by parapets of smooth shining black stone. On those stone seats I sat cross-legged, solving tedious sums, deciphering phrases and idioms. On a wooden chair, which had a funny carved headrest, he sat majestically wielding his power over me. Beyond a bland nod, he never recognised my Herculean attempts to prove myself. Perhaps that was why, this morning, when my cousin told me about my ailing schoolmaster, I did not, or could not, respond immediately.

I was back home on annual leave after my first posting out of my state. I had missed my family, my friends, and my favourite haunts - the beaches and the waterways. A feast of summer fruit – custard apples, country mangoes and palm fruits – was there for me to glut on. The old schoolmaster was not even on the periphery of my thoughts. In the evening, my aunt reminded me once again of the old man. Very old, sick and lonely, practically without a penny, kept by one of his reluctant sons, he was slowly sinking. It was my duty to visit him.

I remember, even in those days, he was a poor man. It was obvious, not the pupil, but the sumptuous meals offered by us, were his main attraction to the house. As the breakfast arrived for both of us, for me, frothy milk laced with almonds and for him, four round idlis, smooth and snowy, floating like submarines in a ruddy pool of sambar, I would surreptitiously watch the gleam in his eyes. As soon as the breakfast tray was laid before him, with quick anxious fingers he would flick the idlis expertly into his mouth. Within minutes, he would down the idlis and the sambar and evince his relish with a brief burp. Once the ritual of his breakfast was over, he would turn his disapproving eyes to me.

'Do you know, there are thousands of kids in this city who can never dream of milk? And you, sulking over a silver mug of milk!' He hissed the words as though he was pronouncing a curse on me. In a sonorous voice, he painted before me a ghastly scene, a scary picture: those half-naked kids greedily drinking chalk-white kanji, poured out in coconut shells – with make-shift spoons, fashioned out of the leaves of the jack fruit tree. Those one-eyed, two-eyed coconut shells, the skull-shaped grinning coconut shells and the leafy spoons haunted me even in my dreams. I felt vaguely sad. I felt vaguely guilty and I hated the old schoolmaster.

A distant cousin of mine who came home to spend her summer vacation from the big city, made all the youngsters dance around her. I was one of her ardent admirers. She was a delicate well-groomed girl. On her dusky oval face there was a small birthmark, triangular shaped, covered with black soft hair. She kept her nails so clean that they shone like freshly washed shells. When she laughed there was a ripple on her downy mole and I couldn't take my eyes off her. Her slightest wish was a command to us.

So we went round the ponds, across the fields, to catch butterflies for her. I still remember those makeshift nets used by us to trap the beautiful winged creatures. A discarded mosquito net used for one of the babies at home came handy. It was like an umbrella which could be snapped shut or open. Each one of us, vying with each other, went on a hunting spree for butterflies of brilliant shades--- bright yellow, deep purple, speckled and spotted, glossy and smooth. The budding researcher, my young cousin, dipped them one by one, in some mysterious solution and pinned them against a board, which had an attractive velvet cover in royal blue.

One afternoon, as I was skipping around the compound on the errands of my lady, the old schoolmaster caught me unaware. The half-moon of the head of his umbrella came down on my neck like a loop. 'Taking those innocent beings to their cross?'

He jeered at me. The beautiful butterfies, in front of my very eyes, turned into giant sinister shapes and I could see them wriggling helplessly on a board. How I shuddered at the ugly sharp pins which went straight through their heart piercing them! I was furious with the old schoolmaster. Why did he have to make me feel so very foolish and small? Crestfallen, I slunk back to my stone seat where he was waiting for me ominously.

On Sunday afternoons, I used to see him sitting in the hall across the chess table, engrossed in a game with my father. My father was always relaxed and happy, especially on a holiday. He would often whistle for us. For my sister and me, that was the green signal which meant that we could join him. Being the youngest, I was always the privileged one. I would cosily settle on his lap and watch him manipulate his pawns. But the old schoolmaster never looked at any one of us. He played so seriously, as though his very life was at stake. His bespectacled eyes would be glued to the black and white chessboard and he sat in studied concentration like a statue of Patience. My sister and I were convinced that he was there for the special holiday lunch. As I moved on to high school, my tuition was discontinued. I used to see him occasionally on festival days like Onam or Vishu, or on some festive occasions of the family.

It was not easy to find his humble home. I did not know what drove me on my mission, crossing railway lines, picking my way through orchards and groves, climbing over pineapple fences, I reached the small red brick house. A bearded man with stained teeth came to the veranda and made me sit on a floor mat. He must be the son, I thought to myself. Somewhere from the back of the house, came the unnerving sound of a persistent cough. I was lead to the rear of the house to a narrow, dingy dark cell of a room. It must have been built as a storeroom of sorts.

As my eyes got used to the darkness around, I saw him at the far end of the room, stretched on a string cot. A bag of bones, he lay there, surrounded by filth and flies. Was he the same formidable old man who introduced me to Jesus Christ and Karl Marx? The spittoon, kept by the side of the cot had overturned. A huge fly was buzzing around the mess it had made on the cracked floor. As the son shouted my name into his ears, he turned towards me. I could trace, in those glassy eyes, a flicker of recognition. He raised a wasted hand with arthritic fingers. Was it a blessing? Was it a recognition which he had held from me so grudgingly all these years? He tried to speak. But his voice was caught in a fresh spasm of cough. I stepped out of the room.

His son followed me with a look of expectancy. I sensed his rightful demand. Taking out a couple of crisp hundred rupee notes from my wallet and slipped them into his waiting hands. As I turned away, I heard him murmur that a film star, an old student of the master had recently sent him a giant sum of one thousand rupees. He was obviously weighing my gesture of kindness. Could he have had any inkling of that giant debt which I still owed to my master?

Trying to put the scene behind, I walked hastily. But the gurgling sound of the cough trapped in the throat, and the wheezing of my master's troubled breathing followed me over the pineapple fences, beyond the railway line to the beach resort where I had planned a bachelors' meet. Flustered, I fled to my freedom. Or was my mind still fettered? I did not quite know.

The Rooster and the Hen

After months of scouting and hunting, I came up on the house. It was tucked away behind one of those busy, important roads of the city. A cool, high-ceilinged bungalow surrounded by shady trees and an unkempt garden, a walking distance from my workplace. Straight from the Registrar's office, we drove down to the house. Malini's parents and mine were only too willing to set us up in a plush flat, in a posh locality. But we would hear none of it. It didn't matter; we had only a big bath-attached room and a strip of a veranda at the rear portion of the building. When I gave our address as 12 Jai Singh Road, rear portion, I felt good even though it was discriminatingly demarcated – the *rear*. After all it was our own dwelling. Father and mother said it was heartless on my part to have rejected their plea to bring the bride home, as was the custom.

Rituals and customs, all sentimental stuff, I am sick of them. Hollow words! Bourgeois hypocrisy! I will raise a family on different lines. Mother says I will change though. She reminds me of my tavarish days. After gruelling sessions of *self-examination* and *self-criticism* with the comrades, I had gone on a rampage in Mamma's beautiful garden, uprooting green grass and flowering plants. Until my hands bled, I had pulled at the roots which had carved a criss-cross of veins under the earth. Those were the days when I had dreamt of a new earth and a new heaven in the order of Lenin and Mao. As a fifteen-year-old hardcore activist, I wanted to replace grass and flowers with *cabbages and cotton*. Now, people tauntingly quote perestroika and Tiananmen Square in my presence. Russia and China are not my conscience keepers. The leaps and falls of giants do not rattle me. I have my own convictions and visions.

A one-room dwelling! How can I cook, sleep, and receive guests, in a single room? Vallabh says, cook in the veranda. That means, parading myself in front of the prying eyes of dhobis, maalis, and sweepers. Of course, I do spend half the day staring at them simply because our home looks straight into the servants' block. That was something Vallabh had not bargained for. Perhaps he was so anxious to settle the accommodation that he didn't think of the ugly rows of these one-roomed shacks, directly facing the back portion of the building. He does feel bad about it. But we cannot afford to leave the house as yet.

Vallabh doesn't call these shacks servant quarters. He has christened them *satellite* houses. I don't know why. I know they exist on the borrowed strength of the bureaucrat housed in the bungalow. But most of these domestic helps have planted themselves here as permanent fixtures— for decades. Basanti, the sweeper tells me, the old tailor staying in one of the quarters has been here for the past four decades. As a young man he had stitched shirts and smocked gowns for the British family which had lived here during colonial time. Babujis come and go once in three or four years, but the dhobis and sweepers are here to stay.

Finally, I decided to design the kitchen in the bedroom itself. I divided the big room with a decorative screen, into two neat sections—a kitchen corner and a cosy sleeping- shrine. A table lamp by the side of the bed and a brass flower vase. The room now looked pleasant enough. I knew Vallabh would frown at me. He wanted a place to live, he said, not a museum for displaying acquisitions. He wanted me to make only functional arrangements; he always reminded me, aesthetics should not be our priority.

Yet, when I turned the veranda with its flimsy jafery door, painted in a cool shade of green, into a mini sitting room, Vallabh was not too unhappy. He helped me pull together three huge tin trunks. I fixed a few padded cushions on them and covered them with a flowery sheet and there it was – a functional seat and a beautiful settee! It is now Vallabh's favourite seat. He spends his mornings huddled on it. His hands wrapped around the tall mug of tea, he enjoys planning his day ahead.

The new tenants at the back seem to be decent folks. The old Spinster, the drawing teacher at the government school, had lived here more than twelve years. When Bablu's papa had brought me to the quarters as a bride... that was twelve years ago, she was there. I cleaned the room and washed clothes for her. And whenever she had her rheumatic attacks, I used to massage her legs and back with herbal oils. "Basanti, there is magic in your hands," she used to tell me. But what a miser she was! She wouldn't give me a pie more than fifty rupees, which was the salary fixed ten years ago. The new memsaheb is young and kind. She has promised to pay me two hundred rupees. She tells me, she got married only last month.

I can't believe it. She wears no jewellery, not even bangles on her wrists. No sindoor. No new clothes. I have never seen her in a sari. She always wears slacks and shirts like a man. I told her this would not do. If you want to keep your man, you must take care of your looks. I don't know why she went into a fit of laughter.

You should have seen Basanti's face when I told her I had brought from my parents' house, neither jewellery nor any trousseau. In fact, I had refused to carry with me the utensils, the furniture, the quilts and the embroidered sheets my mother had been hoarding for me ever since I was born. She sat down on the floor with the mopping cloth, her mouth wide open, 'Saheb took you without any dahej ? And his parents? Had they not demanded any thing?' She refused to believe it. What do you think marriage is? An exchange of cattle? Dahej!. My foot! You think I would allow my parents to buy a bridegroom for me? She wasn't prepared— and I knew it went above and beyond her head- for one of those fiery speeches I am so used to making at the women's development centre.

I don't like the idea of Basanti working in the house. After all, a one room boarding and lodging is something Malini and I should be able to manage ourselves. But Malini says Basanti is so hard up, she needs money to feed her four children and her loafer husband. She is too proud to take anything free. We are only providing employment for her. Well. That is a heartening thought. But for Malini, here is an excellent opportunity. She does not have to step out of the gate to complete her project work on dalit women. All the data is right here, in these one-roomed shacks!

Vallabh says I am unnecessarily getting involved with Basanti. Take her up only as your case history, he tells me. But Basanti is such a dear thing. Her quarter is nearest to our veranda. So I see her everyday. Her day starts at five every morning, summer or winter, rain or storm. She scrubs her brass vessels with charcoal and sand until they shine and neatly puts them away in a wire basket to dry.

Then she goes straight to the night jasmine tree and shakes the flower-laden branches. Delicately scented tiny flowers. Pearly white petals on burnt-orange stems. They have just one night's life! By morning they are grounded, spreading a coral and pearl carpet under the tree. Basanti told me the flowers fallen on the ground are not to be taken for pooja. So, she would collect them in her pallav. The flowers, safely tucked in the folds of her pallav, and a bowl of milk in her hands, she would set out to the nearby Shiva shrine. All married women must worship Shiva, she told me once, and should do abhishek, bathe the Shivaling with milk. That was the right way to ensure long life for one's husband, she told me as though she was warning me!

I wonder why she wants that brute of a husband to live long. When I see her fawning around such a useless man--- simply because he has given her the status of a married woman--- my blood boils. For days and days, he roams around the city, gambling and drinking. Yet, when he comes home, she treats him like a king. She lays a feast to welcome him! Whenever she comes to borrow cloves and cinnamon from me, I know the prodigal husband has returned. She wants to make chicken korma for him! All that she had saved during the entire month, sweeping and swabbing the bungalows of babujis, would go into that one meal. She would place the shining brass thali on an embroidered red scarf and place the delicacies—a mound of rice, puris puffed into golden domes, daal and curries. She would then spread a durry on the floor and the children would conduct him to his seat. Basanti would be sitting a few feet away and fanning—I always wondered whether she was fanning her husband or driving away flies from the thali.

Babloo, Bittu and Guddi would squat around their father and solemnly watch him chewing the chicken bones and smacking his lips. If he left a few pieces of chicken, Bittu and Babloo would fall on them. I asked Basanti why the children were never allowed to join the feast. The man of the house must eat first. And then the boys would eat. Whatever was left, the girls should eat. Basanti had the answer ready.

As night fell, I would hear screams and yells from Basanti's quarters. The next morning, I would see her limping around with her limbs beaten black and blue. And the vagabond of a husband would have once again taken to the road. Basanti takes every thing as her fate, as if nothing can ever be changed. What a miserable lot! Before I leave this house, I must rescue Basanti.

Padlock on the jafery door? I have not taken the duplicate key with me. I never felt the need for it.

Malini hardly ever goes anywhere without telling me. It is half past six. In fact, an hour later than my usual time. Why am I feeling so piqued? Do I expect my wife to stand at the door, straining her ears for the footsteps of her lord and master? What is happening to me? Is Basanti's tale slowly worming its way into my mind? I must say I feel a bit envious of her loafer husband. The fellow doesn't have to raise one little finger. Pampered by his wife and children, fed with delicacies; he is a real emperor in his hut.

Sitting on the floor fanning him and his food, furtively, throwing sidelong glances, even the plain-faced portly Basanti looks charming. How would Malini look with a red bindi on her broad forehead, and the sari thrown over her head? Like a full moon, no like the fourteenth day moon. But how can there be a day-moon? Oh, I have got my aesthetics and logistics, all wrong. I must say lyrically, in the native way *chaudh-vin ka chand.*

I had planned to be back before Vallabh returns. But the temple was so crowded. And Basanti insisted we should wait for the arti. I enjoyed the colourful crowd, the kirtan, the bells and the flickering oil lamps. It was like a psychedelic dell. What a thing to say about the temple! I hardly looked at the idol. Catch me praying! In fact, when Basanti pleaded with me to accompany her, I simply didn't have the heart to say no.

I was worried though. What would Vallabh have to say when he saw me all decked up? Yet, I must say, when I looked at the mirror I thought the bindi didn't look too bad on me. And my unusually long neck definitely looked far better with a string of pearl around it. A little bit of beautification – why should it be an eyesore to any one? As I walked in, I saw Vallabh's face anxiously looking into mine. Did I imagine a flash of admiration in his eyes? Seeing your husband's face on the day of karva chauth, after spotting the moon, Basanti had told me, is very auspicious. I felt strangely elated.

Memsaheb tells me I should send Guddi to school. If she goes to school, who will look after the baby when I am off to work? Memsaheb doesn't know Guddi goes to wash the utensils in two houses two streets away. When I told her Babloo's Papa wants to take the boys off school to send them to the carpet factory in Punjab, she threw such a tantrum! She said she would inform the police and we would be punished for making children work. It seems there is rule that children below fifteen should not be sent to work. How can I make her understand? For us more children mean more hands for work? Am I going to make Babloo and Bittu collectors? She says I am not giving enough food to Guddi. I told her girls should not be pampered. Who knows what is in store for them? Memsaheb says I have got everything wrong in my mind.

She tells me my hard-earned money is not to be given away to Babloo's Papa. It is true he blows it up, gambling and drinking. But how can I refuse him? He beats me to pulp. Last time he came home, I said I had no money. And it was a fact. Whatever I had earned weaving baskets at the centre where Memsaheb goes, I had handed over to her, and she had put it in the bank. But he ransacked the rice tin and toppled the flour sack, the usual places where I hide money and then threatened me if I did not stop working for Memsaheb he would kill me. Someone had been filling his ears. Memsaheb always tells me I should fight back. But the house where a woman raises her voice, is it not doomed forever? That was what my grandmother and my mother used to say. My mother-in-law had told me the same thing.

'All of them have been telling you lies,' Memsaheb screamed at me.

I don't know how to save Basanti. This time, her husband had come home with a girl. He told the dhobi, she was his niece. But everyone knew he was bluffing. Vallabh tells me, he had seen him suspiciously sauntering near Jyoti cinema. Someone had told him he was a pimp.

When I heard the loud wailing of Basanti, I just couldn't control myself. I rushed to their quarters. Her husband was sitting cross-legged on the charpai outside the room as though nothing was wrong with anyone at home. The girl, who sat by his side, stared at me and giggled. The man faced me with a kind of contempt against which, I felt awkward and defenceless.

'You have come to tempt my wife away? Bring the police. Bring all those slogan-screaming women from your blessed centre. Let us see who will win?' He looked me up and down as though he was sizing me up. So bold, so brazen! I was shocked. I saw him getting up insolently to pull up his short frame with glee, as though he knew exactly how to deal with me. It was I who did not know how to deal with him. I stepped back impulsively. Basanti was standing near the window. Her face looked red and swollen as though a beehive had broken loose and descended on her.

'Memsaheb, you told me I should protest. I told him, I won't let him take the boys off school, and I won't send them to Punjab. I won't let this slut in. Look, what he has done to me! Get away Memsaheb, leave this house and go. I don't trust this man. He can harm you.' ... I heard her wailing after me.

Malini told me about her harrowing misadventure with Basanti's husband. She shouldn't have worked herself up. Especially now, as she is right into her fifth month. I am quite upset. But I am glad Malini has realised all those enforcement schemes are not as simple as they are made to sound on the podiums. How am I going to tell her? Our landlord, the bureaucrat has asked us to vacate the house? She would jump to the conclusion that it has something to do with the morning's mishap. Yes, now that I think of it, it is possible somebody might have complained...

'Malini, You know my Maasi's flat, the one who has gone to Canada, is lying vacant. Why don't we move into that flat? You will soon need somebody to help you. How can we keep a maid here?'

'Maid?' Malini raised her shapely eyebrows.

'Okay... Malini, I won't say maid... hmm- we need a domestic help.' Malini looked hard at me, obviously not very impressed. It took me almost one week to convince her.

Malini sorted out the clothes and the kitchen stuff and I piled books and files into cartons. As I was separating the trunks and dismantling the settee on the veranda, I heard the shouts and yells outside. The dhobi and his son, Babloo and Bittu were all on the run. With sticks and poles in hands, they were chasing someone. Who were they chasing? I called out to them.

'Babuji it is the hen,' Dhobi shouted back. 'One of the hens has crowed. You know only roosters must crow. It is not natural. It is a bad omen. Something terrible may happen. We must kill this hen.'

A hen crowing? Nonsense. I knew for sure, it was one of their antics to scare Basanti. '*Pakado, pakado, pakado...* Catch her, catch her...They were at it again. I could see the poor hen running for her life. Scrambling over the spinach field, she even tried to lift herself up on to the roof. She failed and fell on the ground. At last, near the fence, one of the boys caught her. A frantic flutter, a squeak, a thud – the hen lay limp and lifeless on the flowerbed.

Kokaree... ko.... The rooster, seated theatrically on the tin roof of the poultry shed, crowed – a single triumphant call. The red flower on his head gleamed like a crown against the twilight. The hens enclosed in the shed, huddled together and clucked ominously in chorus. I drew the curtains and shut the green jafery door firmly behind. Good, Malini had not come out. It wouldn't have been a good sight for a woman who was expecting her first child.

Window

The high-rise buildings and condominiums were far too many. But to come across a luxury apartment, right in the heart of the city, was indeed an incredible stroke of luck. Nestling on a hillock, surrounded by lush-green trees of oil palm, the Sylvan Heights apartments were just the ultimate anyone would wish for. An artfully laid rugged rocky path. It almost looked like a jungle trail. It conveniently connected the apartments to the tree-lined boulevard that encircled the city— this city of eternal summer— like a green girdle. It did not matter if the apartment had cost Joy's parents a fortune?

It was the elaborate three sided ornamental window of the drawing room, with its gabled canopy rising majestically on the outer wall, which gave the apartment an exclusive and classy look. As Joy's mother claimed, it was an architectural marvel. No other flat in the condominium had such an intricate structure. The sleek, compact, functional windows, ideally designed to suit the high-rise buildings did not appeal to Mother. She insisted on restructuring them. It was a massive job. Father was against it. But ultimately, as usual, he gave in. A window on a fourth floor apartment did not need any ugly grille. Yet, for Joy's safety, his mother got a lattice-like frame attached to it from inside.

For Mother, the beautiful window with its geometrical motifs-delicately etched on the glass panes—was something to brag about. But for Joy, it meant a lot more. For him, it was a window with a view. It overlooked the rear boundary walls of the building, beyond which extended a mini jungle harbouring varieties of reptiles and monstrous looking monitor lizards. During sunny afternoons, Joy had seen these huge scaly lizards coming out into the clearing and lying lazily on the grass. The land where the condominium had come up, had once been a shantytown. The small wooden house of Sethu, built on stilts, standing on the outskirts of the jungle, was now the lone surviving shanty in the vicinity. Joy knew the inmates of that house almost intimately, though he had not visited them even once.

Seated on the windowsill, he had spent long afternoons and evenings watching the family, following them with his eyes. Sethu was a petty vendor. A swarthy dark giant of a man with a square face and a bushy salt-and-pepper moustache, he went round the city on a moped wearing a weather-beaten steel helmet, and sold bread, buns and biscuits. When he returned home after his daily rounds, the whole family would come out and give the master of the house a ceremonious welcome. Selvam and Siva, his two young sons, reverently took charge of the moped. One of them would park the moped in the tin shed where they stored firewood and chicken feed. If Siva wiped the moped and washed the muddy tyres, Selvam would help his father carry the bags inside.

Sethu's wife, a short stout woman, dressed in a sarong and a loose blouse, stood with her baby daughter in her arms and fretted around her husband. Keen to climb on to her father's shoulders, the little girl would try to break out of her mother's arms. Joy held his breath when Sethu tossed the baby up in the air. Like an expert juggler he would catch her and the child would cling to him and laugh. How happy they looked! Joy watched the scene wistfully.

Before Joy's mother took up her job in the cosmetic firm, hadn't she spent all her time with Joy? Joy didn't have any brothers. Nor did he have any sisters. So what? He grew up as Mamma's and Papa's joy. A hundred times, Mamma had told him ever so fondly, what a darling baby he had been. A bouncing, bubbling bundle of Joy. Playful, active—that was how Mamma had described him. It was only natural, they chose to call him Joy. Even now at the age of nine Joy looked so cute. A mop of soft black hair that spilled mischievously over his forehead, and his eyes shining like a pair of beads – wasn't he an angel of a child? Not only his parents, even neighbours and friends adored him.

When mother was at home, time just flew – in a swirl of activities. Joy remembered the Mah-jong mornings at home. A bevy of ladies, from the neighbouring flats, would flock around their drawing room. Joy enjoyed helping his mother while she got the room ready. After all Mamma was a house-proud person. What did that mean? Joy didn't have the faintest idea. A well-dressed lady who visited them once – Joy remembered her crane-like neck and her darting eyes– had said so. Mother seemed very pleased to hear that. That was how Joy came to believe that his mother was house-proud. With his tiny hands he polished the low lacquer tables until they shone and one could see one's reflection on them. Spider-shaped orchids of a deep purple shade, Mother's favourite, arranged in the blue and white porcelain vase, looked fresh and beautiful. Filling tiny crystal bowls with dry fruit and candies, was something Joy really enjoyed.

When the ladies sat across the Mah-jong table

indulging themselves in a game of gamble– a harmless one, for the stake was only a few cents – Joy sat in his own room and practised on his piano. A soft rising melody swept over the house as a suitable background for the Mah-jong party. The ladies who came for the party were constantly chatting. Mostly they grumbled, either about their husbands or about their maids.

Some of them good-humouredly complained about their naughty children. Auntie Jasmine narrated the pranks of her three-year-old son in her typical hilarious way. While she was on a visit to the country cottage of her mother-in-law, the child wanted to take eggs from the wire basket that was hanging in the kitchen, and insisted on dashing them on the floor one by one. Aunt Minnie told them, in her singsong voice how her darling daughter once went on a rampage in a shop in Chinatown because she was refused her thirteenth Barbie doll. Joy heard his mother's clear ringing voice above the din of the gossip and laughter. Joy never embarrassed her anywhere. She couldn't remember a time when Joy had thrown such temper tantrums. Mother's friends cooed in chorus, 'You should be proud of your Joy.' Yes, Joy had always been, and was, even today, at the tender age of nine, a gentleman-child.

When Mother drove away with Father in a brisk and busy way, planting a brief kiss on his forehead, did Joy ever protest? Of course Joy was not at all pleased with the arrangement. But then he never made a scene. He stayed at home with the trained maid Mamma had specially chosen for him, had his meals, went to school, played games and as dusk fell, sat himself cosily on the window-sill and waited patiently for his parents to come home.

Some days, Joy would watch with amusement, a change of scene at the shanty. Sethu would be hanging around the house. Lying on a cot, under the mango tree he would sleep and sleep. When the boys came home from school, he would join them in a game of marbles or the trio would walk to the open space behind the condominium to fly kites. Those were the times when Joy had an opportunity to see them at close quarters. He would go down, on the pretext of going to the swimming pool and would stay back to witness their kite race. Sethu would laugh and shout, throw his hands up and down urging them to fly the kites higher and higher. At times, he would abuse them. If one of them cut the kite of the other, he would mediate between them so affectionately. With rapt attention,

Joy would watch the scene. The rustling sound of the paper kites as they went up with the breeze, the sound of the running feet of the children, their laughter, their shouts, always fascinated him.

A little dazed, he would go back to his apartment and pull down his toys, one by one. He owned the latest toys in the market: hi-tech electronic toys, video games, computer games. He only had to name a game. His father would scour supermarkets, or even place postal orders to get them home. There it was. The race car set. Yes, he could do with a car race. But who would race with him? Of course, the maid. She was the only one at home who could play with him. Joy would drag her out of the kitchen, forcing her to leave the soup and the lamb chops behind. But she was no match to him. He won every game or did she let him win? No thrill at all!

Bored, and sullen, he would turn to his computer and load one of his latest combat games. Violence was far from the mind of mild-mannered Joy. But in the realm of virtual reality, he could afford a few lapses. There was no harm in shooting down a few monsters, dragons, warriors or thieves. On and on his mouse clicked, merrily, mischievously, almost vengefully. Down, down went those figures, one by one - Sethu –

Siva—Selvam came down with a thud, lifeless in a heap. What victory! What thrill!

As evening came, once again he retreated to the window, and waited for his parents. What a relentless spell of rain it was! One full week, almost without a pause. How Joy hated the last four days! Trapped indoors, it was miserable. Standing near the window, he had listened to the fury of the rain as it came lashing down against roofs, awnings, beams and the treetops. The monotonous sound was occasionally punctuated by peals of thunder. A depressing dark blanket of rain had blurred the view of the jungle and the shanty. What a relief, to wake up to a bright day! Washed by rain, the air outside looked pristine crisp and fresh. The leaves on the trees were smooth and shiny. The grass glistened as though it wore drops of diamonds.

Joy's eyes wandered, almost instinctively, to the shanty. What could have happened? So many people! What were they doing at Sethu's house? Silent and solemn they stood in small groups around the house. Something was wrong. Something was terribly wrong. Joy knew at once. His eyes frantically searched for Selvam and Siva. Yes, they were there. But where was Sethu? He was nowhere to be seen. Sethu's wife was sitting on the ground near the tin shed with her head buried in her arms. At some distance stood a bier, holding a coffin, laden with marigold and roses. Two elderly men stepped forward and gently lifted the bier. A few more joined them. Selvam and Siva helped their mother to her feet. She was weeping uncontrollably. The boys supported her from either side and they moved in behind those men.

The maid who was busy swabbing the floor threw her mop down and came rushing to the window. Hastily she pulled Joy away from his seat.

'Don't have to see all that. Don't you know Sethu died yesterday? No..... No...... He was not on his moped. He was standing under a tree to protect himself from the rain. The heavy branches of the tree broke loose and crashed on his head. He died on the spot.'

Joy blinked at the maid. What was she blubbering about? Sethu, who doted on Selvam, Siva and the little girl, is dead? Oh no! Joy felt a lump in his throat. Sethu is no more! How many times, naughty and wicked, had he shot him down on the computer screen? Had he wished him dead? The maid put a comforting arm around the sobbing child.

Hush, hush. Such things do happen. It could have happened to anyone. It is God's will. She spoke softly, stroking his hair. Joy wiped his tears and looked at Susie, not too sure of himself. A pair of kind eyes and a lop-sided smile, Susie had never looked so dear or dignified. He buried his head into her apron – smelling of detergents and lotions--- and hugged her gratefully.

Mirage

I know what name we should give him. The booksays, the name of a dog should ideally start with a consonant. A harsh authoritative sound so that the dog would respond immediately. Yes. That is it. We shall call him Sando.'

'Sando? What nonsense! You want to make him a mindless body builder? Lily, your mind can go only that far!'

'As if Neil, you are a philosopher-poet! How are you sure dogs have minds? I am the youngest and it is my privilege to name this teeny-weeny thing.'

The teeny-weeny thing sat cosily on a straw bed in the cane basket. Rejecting Neil's outstretched hands, it withdrew to the farthest corner of the basket. Putting out a tiny pink tongue, it licked the rim of the basket and with its crystal bead eyes, looked straight at Lily.

'See he has eyes only for me, not for you. Poor thing. Aren't you tired travelling all day in the train my sweetie pie? Did Bahadur take good care of you?'

'Do you think Granny would spare Bahadur if he didn't? Look at the packets, Granny has sent. Meals and medicines. Each packet is clearly marked – morning, afternoon, evening and night. Granny is so organised! Forget Bahadur. Let us settle on a name first. I think we should call him Brownie after his colour.'

'Oh Neil, how can you? It smacks of.... Shall I tell you what? As Dad says, a *colonial hangover.*'

' I bet you don't know the meaning of what you're saying Lily. If you could kindly educate me as to the meaning of such a big word?'

'Why should I? You are a brown sahib. Yes, that is what you are.'

'Is that another big word you have learnt?'

'I know what I should call my dog. Hmm.... Candy is a good name isn't it? That sounds good. Candy, Candy!'

'Candy! I am shocked. Why don't you call him Lollipop? Your friends will say, how *chweet*! I can imagine. Think of a manly name. How about Brutus? It is a harsh sounding name and it has the sanction of Shakespeare.'

'Ugh! You will give him the name of a Betrayer?'

'What's in a name? Call him Lucifer (That was Rishi. The pandemonium had brought him down from his ivory tower, his study room)'

'Oh Dad! Why do you say that? Is our home a hell that needs to be guarded by a Lucifer? At least don't say it in Mama's hearing. Come on. Dad! You suggest a name. You know Lily and I cannot agree on anything.'

'Susan! Why don't you come down and help the children? You didn't have any problem finding names for your children. Now, here is a challenge for you.'

True, Rishi and Susan didn't have to rack their brains to find suitable names for their children. The daughter would be named after Susan's mother Elizabeth and the son after Rishi's father, Neelkanth Sharma. Even before their marriage had taken place, it had been settled. That Elizabeth was shortened to Lily and Neelkanth to Neil was only natural, a development in tune with the secular set up of their family.

When Susan and Rishi fell in love, it had caused quite a stir. Family and friends vociferously voiced the usual apprehensions and doubts. Rishi, from an orthodox Brahmin family from down south, somewhere near Cape Comorin and Susan, from a forward Anglo Indian family from Dehradun at the foothills of the Himalayas. The disparity was too conspicuous and alarming. So they said. But the lovers ultimately—as it always happens --- had their own way. They knew they were made for each other and they were sure religion, language and background --- all this was stuff and nonsense. Church and temple were insignificant in the face of the marriage of true minds.

As Susan came down, three pairs of admiring eyes were turned to her. Wiping her paint-stained hands on her multicoloured apron—she had been working on her easels all morning—she settled down on the floor in front of the new arrival.

'Yes, I will christen our little pet.'

'Mama, will you baptise him?'

Rishi looked severely at the threesome. But the three were so captivated by the teeny-weeny thing that they did not notice Rishi's frown. True, religious terms were normally banned in the house. But on such extraordinarily happy situations there could be slips and omissions. It was no major offence against the discipline of the house!

'I am going to give him an unusual name. We will call him Mirage.'

'Are you out of your mind Susan? Mirage means something. Do you think it is a name like Neeraj or Dheeraj?'

'Of course I know. You cannot challenge my vocabulary. Who beats you at the Scrabble? And I am surprised Rishi, don't you know Dheeraj and Neeraj also mean something. You, the son of a Sanskrit Pundit, I can't believe it!'

Mirage, by now, had become used to the sound and

the smell of the house. He gingerly got out of the basket and tottered around Rishi and Susan, licked Neil's big toes and settled on Lily's lap.

Bahadur remembered the scene, every detail of it as though it had happened only the other day. How time had flown! Mirage was now four years old. What had not happened in these four years? Animals, he had been told, have an uncanny memory. In Nepal, in his native village, he had heard of vindictive tigers, vengeful snakes and clever monkeys. Mirage must have a sharp memory. In his sleep, he moaned, grunted and cried. He must be remembering Susan and Rishi and of course, the children. The children were away at boarding school in Dehradun. Rishi and Susan were still at home. But what was the use? No one knew what time Rishi would come home, what time he would leave. As for Susan she was most of the time touring, one month in London, one month in America. God only knew where all she went, carrying with her crates and crates of paintings.

Poor Mirage! Every morning, he would pick up the newspaper and push his way into their room. Rishi wouldn't even care to open his eyes. He would shout for Bahadur to take Mirage away. Bahadur remembered the good old days when Sahib and the children got up at the crack of dawn and took Mirage to the nearby park for a walk. Neil carried an old cycle tyre with him and made Mirage jump through it as though through a Ring of Fire. Tempting him with biscuits, he made him do all kinds of tricks. How Lily used to fight with her brother!

'Don't you treat Mirage as though he is a circus dog? Stop being a ringmaster,' Lily would scream at Neil. Father and children would come home singing and shouting, with Mirage close at their heels or running ahead of them with his tail curled at the back. Bahadur, who always waited for them in the garden with a steaming pot of tea, used to feel happy just looking at them.

Mirage still performed tricks. He would take the tyre up and down the corridor, run in and out of Neil's room. Occasionally, he would pause in his tracks and look around as though he expected Neil and Lily to applaud him. Who says dogs have no minds? When Mirage realised there was no one watching him, he would sheepishly curl his tail and walk back to the kennel.

The kennel was one of the recent additions to the house. When the rooms in the house were closed for Mirage, it was Bahadur who had suggested that Rishi build a dog's house. In the good old days, Mirage slept in the dining hall near Lily's aquarium. When Lily dropped powders and grains to the fish, he would demand his favourite chocolate wafers from her. He would sit and stare hard at the multicoloured fish swirling around under the water rockery and bark at them occasionally, as though they were his rivals. When Lily left for boarding school she presented the aquarium to one of her friends. Thank God! Or else, Bahadur who had a hundred and one jobs to do would have had to deal with the corpses of the fish as well.

Beside the aquarium, Bahadur remembered how Mirage had posed for his portrait, majestically seated on his hind legs on the quilted rug which Susan had specially made for him. That was one of Susan's masterpieces. It now stood on the wall facing the dining table. Now and then, Mirage would stand before the portrait and bark his protest. Bahadur could do nothing but gently coax him to move away.

Mirage was rolling on the grass outside the kennel. With one front leg up in the air, with the paws of his other leg, he was trying to scratch his under belly.

What a funny sight! Bahadur couldn't help laughing. He noticed that the fawn furry coat, which was once smooth and glossy, had now turned into a dull brown and was dotted here and there with ticks. Though Bahadur bathed and brushed the dog regularly, how could be so meticulous and caring like Susan? If Susan found one tick on Mirage, she would bring the entire house down. Bahadur could never forget the operations she used to conduct on Mirage—with sterilised tweezers she would pull out the ticks one by one, and then she would douse Mirage with antiseptic lotions.

Susan had now found an easy way to deal with the tick problem. When she went on her foreign tours, she picked up tick collars for Mirage. But it was so strange, nothing ever worked on him. The ticks clung to him as though they were passionately in love with him. After her last trip abroad, when Susan returned home, she was shocked to see ticks crawling all over the house. Of course, she blamed Bahadur for it.

Nowadays, Rishi and Susan found fault with whatever Bahadur did. But Bahadur had no complaints. He had known Susan so long. When he had come to Susan's house as a domestic help, she had been only a schoolgirl and he remembered, he himself was very young – in his early teens. Bahadur's father had worked as a loyal soldier in Indian Army for almost two decades. After retirement, when he returned to Nepal, he had only one ambition to see his son in uniform.

That was how Bahadur had crossed the boundary and had landed in India. Colonel Mathew, Susan's father, did try his best to induct him into the Indian Army. When he was rejected on medical grounds, the Colonel felt sorry for him and gave him a permanent place in his own house. Once a year, preferably in the summer, he would go home to be with his family. His father was no more. But his mother, wife and three children were still in Nepal.

When Susan got married and set up her own home in Delhi, her mother had sent Bahadur along with her. Elizabeth had made it very clear to Bahadur that he was there on her behalf, to take care of her daughter and her family. Bahadur took his duty most conscientiously and had stuck to his post like a sentinel. But the cook and the maid were new to the family. Why should they put up with the temper of Rishi and the tantrums of Susan? In these two years, Bahadur ruefully remembered how many maids and cooks had come and gone. If Susan liked a maid, Rishi was sure to dislike her. If Rishi praised a cook, Susan would boycott him. How long would servants bear the brunt of the petty quarrels of a warring couple? In protest, they had left one by one. Only Bahadur and Mirage remained now, the old faithfuls, to watch and mutely witness the family drama.

Bahadur wondered when all this had started? Was it the day when they, the five of them – Elizabeth had come down to celebrate the second birthday of Mirage – returned from church? As soon as they entered the house, Lily had turned to her mother

'Mama, why did you storm out of the church, dragging us along?'

After the priest concluded the service and came up to them with bread and wine, Elizabeth had abruptly got up and walked out of the church. Susan and Rishi had followed and the children were whisked away too.

'I wanted to taste the wine and the bread,' Lily moaned.

'What a stupid girl! Don't you know you cannot do that because you are not baptised?'

If only Neil had known his innocent remark would spark off a showdown!

'No Neil, there is nothing like that...' Susan's protests

were drowned by Rishi's voice, raised to an unusual pitch.

'So Susan, you do regret— and your mama— that your children are not baptised. You are sad they couldn't eat of the flesh and drink the blood.'

The cutting edge, the bitter tone didn't escape anyone. And Susan's retort was prompt and sharp.

'Rishi, don't you use that mimicking tone? What about the holy water which comes down the drain of your Ganesh temple? You lap it up as theertham.'

Then followed a battle of wit. A loud and ugly scene! Elizabeth and the children withdrew in embarrassment leaving the enraged couple to rave and rant.

Bahadur hated scenes. He remembered the brickbats, back home, between his wife and his mother. He knew his mother had a nasty tongue. But he had always pleaded with his wife to bear with the older woman. He would warn his wife, a war of words would only leave bitterness behind. Every year, when he went on leave he had to face the same scene. He would try in vain to mediate between the two women. He had not seen them for a long time, he reminded himself, a trifle sad. How could he ask for leave when the family was in such a state? He had been, of course, sending money regularly. But money was not everything. His wife had begged him again and again to take her along with him. It was tough putting her off. This time he would bring her. He could surely leave mother for a while with his cousin.

Yes, Bahadur was sure: that petty quarrel over the bread and wine marked the beginning of the end... Oh no! Let it not be the end! He wished and prayed with all his heart. Susan and Rishi argued and fought bitterly whenever they were together. Then, there were the long spells of silence. Rishi spent his evenings in the club. Susan locked herself in the studio and the children roamed around the city with their friends.

When they decided to send the children away to boarding school, Bahadur was not surprised. The house was no longer a home for anyone.

Mirage was the most bewildered creature. No walks, no tricks, no play. Bahadur sadly watched him, trying to pull at Susan's gown, snatching Lily's slippers, and toppling Rishi's books,.... Poor thing, just begging for attention! It was pathetic. But Rishi and Susan, Neil and Lily, each one of them, ignored him and finally he withdrew to his newly built kennel.

The day the children went back to school after the winter vacation, Mirage became almost wild. He broke out of the leash, ran past the gate and chased the car. Bahadur couldn't control him. And then it happened. A speeding motorcycle hit him and he fell across the pavement. One of his front legs was fractured, but luckily he survived the accident. The children postponed their journey and came back from the railway station. Mirage put out his plastered leg to Neil and whimpered as though he was begging him to stay back. He and Lily did stay back until Susan returned from her trip.

Just a day before they left, Mirage got into a strange mood. He wouldn't step out of the kennel. He wouldn't touch food. For two days Mirage kept them on tenterhooks. At last, Rishi and Susan together took him to the hospital. Straightaway, the vet put him on the drip. The children were called back. Susan sat by his side and wept silently. Lily and Neil took turns to massage his legs. Rishi paced up and down the corridor, puffing at his cigarette. At last the four of them were together! A heartening sight thought Bahadur, the least they could do for Mirage! The fractured dog ran his tired eyes on the family-in-waiting, huddled around him.

Bahadur heard Lily asking the vet in a tearful voice,'Doctor, will he survive?'

'Let us hope so. He isn't old. If you take good care of him he should survive.' Neil and Lily kneeled on the floor and prayed. Was it a Christian prayer? Rishi didn't seem to mind. Susan turned to Rishi and said very softly – but Bahadur heard every word of it.

'Mirage should live. Without Mirage, there is no life.'

Bahadur's eyes were brimming. What a relief! Of course, Mirage should survive. And he knew, he would. Now, Susan might grant him his long-postponed leave. His youngest son, who was just learning to walk when he had last been to Nepal – that was two years ago – must be now going to school. It would be great he thought, to be with his family once again.